MY BOSS'S SISTER

MAKE HER MINE SERIES-BOOK 3

ALEXIS WINTER

VALERIE

"It can't be that bad, Val," Maddie, my sister-in-law, says, passing me my third glass of wine.

"You don't know Callan like I do, Mads," I tell her, taking a sip and setting the glass down on the table between us. "He's tortured me my whole life. I wish Bennet could find another place for me," I pout.

She laughs and pulls her feet up onto her deck chair, looking out over their property. There are a couple gardeners in the yard, planting some new plants and taking care of the ones that already alive and thriving.

"What are my two favorite girls up to?" Bennet asks, stepping onto the porch and sitting beside Maddie.

"Having a glass of wine, talking about work," Maddie tells him, leaning up for a quick kiss.

"Is she pouting already? She doesn't even start until tomorrow," he laughs out.

I hold up my middle finger. "It would be like you and Krista working together," I say with a smile.

"Who's Krista?" Maddie asks, looking between the two of us.

"She's Val's best friend since they were five-years-old. She's always had a crush on me, and she would never leave me alone. Drove me crazy," he confesses.

I laugh. "She didn't have a crush on you. She just liked to annoy you. Same with Callan and me. Growing up, neither of us liked the other. He'd call me names and I'd avoid him at all costs."

"Oh, come on," Bennet says. "You're making it sound like you were the angel in all of this."

"I was!" I screech, sitting upright.

He laughs. "Okay, so who was it that taped his underwear to a flag pole?"

"I did, but that was after he stole my clothes from the locker room."

"Who told Michael Gallaway that Callan had a secret crush on him?"

"I did, but that was after he told the whole school that he saw me making out with Krista. To this day, people still think I'm a lesbian. Not that I care. There are worse things to be," I say with a shrug.

He laughs and shakes his head. "So you're saying that everything you've done to him was all in the name of revenge?"

I nod once. "That's right. If he would've left me alone, I would've left him alone." I pick up my glass of wine and take another sip, leaning back and getting comfortable again now that I'm done being attacked by my brother.

"You know, this sounds like a match made in heaven. I bet you two start sleeping together," Maddie says.

"What?" Bennet asks.

"Ew, no way. That's sick. I wouldn't touch him with your vagina and blame it on Bennet," I say, crossing my arms. I want to gag at the thought of sleeping with Callan. Actually, I don't want to think about sleeping with Callan at all. I need to be able to hold down my wine.

"Just wait and see," she says with a smile like she's already planning our wedding or something.

Bennet points at me. "Don't you dare sleep with him. You hear me?" His brows are lifted high, and his eyes are wide and serious.

I hold up my hands. "I've never been surer of anything in my life. Hell will freeze over before I lay a hand on Callan Gregory."

"Alright, I have to get back to work," Bennet says, giving Mads a kiss and standing to go back into the garage.

When he's far enough away, I look over at Mads. "So, how's the whole *I'm going to build race cars and sell them* thing going?"

She smiles. "Really good, actually. I can honestly say I'm surprised by the race car market. I figured he'd build one at a time and wait until it sold before he started on another. But nope, he has like three going in there right now. And they're all sold!" Her blue eyes widen with excitement.

"Wow, that is pretty amazing," I agree. "So, what's the next step for you guys? No baby talk yet?"

She scrunches her nose. "We've talked. I think we've decided against it."

"Really? You mean my brother, the millionaire, doesn't want an heir to his empire?"

She rolls her eyes. "I guess we haven't talked about that. But we've only been married for a year. We have plenty of time to decide what we want. You know, after we enjoy our twenties and settle down a bit. We're still too immature to even think about something as serious as a child."

I laugh. "I'm glad I'm not the only one. I can't believe all these young couples getting married and having babies before they're even old enough to buy a drink. I mean, grow up, enjoy the world before settling down with one person, in one place."

She looks over at me with a wide smile. "I like the way you think. From one non-relationship girl to the other." She holds up her glass of wine and taps it against mine.

"Were you a player too?" I ask.

She rolls her eyes. "I wouldn't call me a player. I mean, players play people to get what they want. I was a straight-up THOT," she jokes with a laugh.

We finish up our bottle of wine as the sun starts to set. Finally, when the temperature drops, we head inside to start on dinner.

"Hey, is it cool if I stay the night and ride in with you guys in the morning? I've had a little too much to drink to drive all the way back to Mom's."

Maddie smiles and nods. "Of course, Val. You know you're always welcome. I mean, what are all these bedrooms for anyway?"

"Thanks," I say with a smile as I continue tossing the salad—the only thing I know how to do when it comes to cooking.

———

WHEN I WAKE up in the morning, I realize that I did not come prepared. I came over to hang out with Mads. Since she and Bennet have gotten married, we've grown close. She's more like a sister that's my best friend than a sister-in-law.

I rush across the hall and knock on their bedroom door. Seconds later, Maddie is opening the door, hair and makeup done, but she's still in her fluffy white robe. "Good morning," she says around a smile.

I lean against the door jam. "So, I'm totally irresponsible, and I don't have anything to wear to work." I offer up an awkward smile.

She laughs and rolls her eyes. "Come on," she says, turning and walking across the room to her closet. She opens the door and we walk into what she calls a closet—I think it's more of a room that holds nothing but clothes. There are racks and racks of clothes, endless drawers, and shelving that holds her shoes and purses. In the center of the room is a circular seating area, and against the far wall is a lit-up vanity.

"Wow, can we say swanky?"

She turns to me with a smile. "I know. Trust me: this wasn't my doing. This is all your brother."

"What did I do?" Bennet walks into the closet, hair wet and slicked back from his shower.

"Designed this closet," Maddie answers.

"I didn't design it; I just let a woman do it while telling her money was no object." He smiles and gives Maddie a quick kiss. "Good morning," he says against her lips before pulling away and grabbing his shoes off the rack. He leaves us alone once again.

Maddie has this dreamy look on her face, and while I think it's utterly disgusting that my brother makes her look that way, I also find it sweet. I can only hope that I'm as happy as her one day.

"Help yourself," she says, taking something down for herself and moving out of the closet.

I walk through and end up choosing a black pencil skirt that ends just below my knee, a light pink shirt that has ruffled short sleeves, and a pair of black pumps. I stand back and look myself over in the mirror.

Everything fits to perfection and hugs my curves nicely. I sit at the vanity and pull my long, dark hair into a bun, with a few strands hanging down to frame my face. I don't want to use any of her makeup, so I rush back into my room to dig things out of the bottom of my purse. Luckily, I find a tube of lipstick and mascara. What more does a girl need?

I'm walking down the stairs the moment they're gathering up their things to leave for the office.

"Are you ready for your first day, Val?" Bennet asks, pulling on his jacket.

I roll my eyes. "No, I'm comparing Callan in his office to the devil sitting on his fiery throne in hell," I joke.

"It can't be that bad, Val," Maddie says, opening the door and motioning for me to walk ahead of her. "Try having a positive attitude about it. Maybe if Callan sees that you're taking the job seriously, so will he. He could be completely different at work."

"I guess," I agree, walking across the porch to the G-Wagon.

The drive to the office isn't a fast one with morning traffic, but it doesn't take nearly long enough for my liking. All too soon, we're pulling into the garage. We all climb out of the car and head toward the elevators. Bennet quickly kisses Maddie and turns to me.

"I'll take you up to his office."

I nod and cross my arms, feeling like a child that's being delivered to the principal's office. I follow behind him as he takes me to the fifth floor and through a set of double doors.

"Callan, look who's here for her first day of work," Bennet says.

5

But I don't pay any attention as I look around his office. The floor is made of shiny black stone, and it's so clean that I can see my white underwear reflecting off it from under my skirt. I pull my legs closer together and look around the office, not wanting to draw Callan's attention to where I'm staring. In the far corner, there's a smaller desk —I'm assuming mine—a seating area with black leather couches, and a glass table between them. There's your typical drink cart, because who doesn't drink alcohol at work, and finally, his massive desk at the head of the room.

I turn in a circle, taking it all in until I'm looking at his smug face. His blond hair is styled nicely. It's not short, but not exactly long either. His blue eyes look me up and down as his lips turn up into a smile.

"This? This is Valerie? Little Valerie?" he asks, walking closer.

"Yeah, she's grown up quite a bit," Bennet says. "Anyway, take it easy on her, will ya?"

"Of course," Callan agrees as Bennet walks out, leaving us alone.

"How ya been, Val?" Callan asks, crossing his arms over his chest and smiling wide.

I roll my eyes and force a smile onto my face. "Great. And yourself?"

He shrugs, smile never fading. "Better now that I have you here to torture." He spins around and heads over to the little desk in the corner. "This is all yours."

"Gee, thanks," I mumble, walking closer and setting my purse down on the top. "What exactly will I be doing?"

"You know, your basic assistant stuff. Fetching my coffee and lunch, filing papers for me, answering the phone, and taking messages. Nothing crazy."

"Great." I slide between the desk and my chair and sit down, looking up at him. I don't know what it is, but just looking at his face makes me angry. He's like a walking Ken doll. He has the perfect blond hair, blue eyes, tan, muscular body. And he's a total playboy. God, just knowing that I have to spend eight hours a day with him has me breaking out in hives. I start scratching my arm.

6

"Still doing that, huh?" He looks down on me with disgust.

"What?" I ask, locking my eyes on his, a little offended.

He uses his right hand to scratch his left arm—making fun of me. "You should get that checked out by a doctor. After all these years, you'd think you'd have some special medication by now."

"I only do it when I'm around you. But I do have that dog allergy, so…"

He fakes a laugh and points at me. "Still just as funny as always."

2

CALLAN

I give Val a list of emails that need to be written up and sent and leave my office. I walk into Bennet's office without being announced, and he looks up at me. His face is slack, and his head is slightly tilted to the side. He knows what's coming.

"I'm not sure about this, man," I say, pouring a drink and sitting down across from him.

"Why? What'd she do?" he breathes out, sounding bored and slightly annoyed.

"She's just…" I start. "She," I try again. "I…" I shake my head.

"So, nothing?" he asks, holding one of his hands palm up.

"No, not nothing. She's mouthy and offensive. She called me a dog," I say, standing up to pace while drinking my beverage.

He laughs. "She what?"

I stop and turn to face him. "She's going to town on her arm, then when I asked what her deal was, she said she has a dog allergy."

Bennet busts out laughing as he shakes his head. "She doesn't have a dog allergy," he says around his laughs.

"Great. I'm not a dog!" I point out, only making him laugh harder.

"Well, maybe she's just allergic to you." He shrugs and stands up. "Either way, you're both adults and have to learn how to work together. Got it?" he asks, placing his hand on my shoulder and leading me toward the door.

"Yeah, but isn't there someplace else you could put her? I can go without an assistant," I offer.

He pushes me through the door. "Nope, sorry." Without another word, he closes the doors between us.

Fuck. I should never have agreed to this. When he said his sister could fill the spot, I was just relieved that I wouldn't have to answer my own phone anymore. I didn't think about having to work with her. She's been a pain in my ass since I was nine. She would always run and tell on Bennet and me for every little thing. To this day, I can hear her high-pitched squeal cutting through me. Just thinking about it causes my ears to ring from the memory.

I walk back into my office, and she looks up. "You got a rather disgusting phone call from Abby."

"What did she want?" I ask, sitting behind my desk.

"Do you want me to read you the message?" she asks, one brow lifted.

I nod. "Go on." I smile, happy to make her comply with my wishes.

She shakes her head once, picks up a notepad, and begins reading. "Callan, I had such a wonderful time with you last night. I can barely walk today! I had no idea you were packing that deadly weapon between your legs. Anyway, call me the next time you're in the mood for a good, dirty fuck." She smiles.

My mouth is hanging open. "She said that to you?"

"Nope. I got it off your voicemail." She smiles and drops the notepad back onto her desk with a thump.

"My private voicemail?" I ask, feeling around my pocket for my cell phone.

She holds my phone up and shakes it. "You need to pick a better password. I mean, your birthday?"

I stand and walk over to her, grabbing the phone from her grip.

"That's the first thing everyone tries."

I slide the phone into my pocket as I walk back to my desk. "I'm just surprised that you care enough to remember my birthday." I smile, thinking I got her.

"How could I forget? You always make such a big deal out of your birthday parties. Every year, it's like you're a teenage girl planning your MTV Sweet Sixteen."

Just the sound of her voice gets under my skin. "Alright, how about we don't talk, huh? Work for you?" I ask. I can hear the strain in my voice from trying not to yell at her. I hope she can too, so she'll stop pushing my buttons.

She closes her mouth and then uses her hand to lock it. Then, she tosses away the key. I scoff and roll my eyes but turn to my computer to get some work done.

———

Noon rolls around, and I write down my lunch order. I walk over to her desk and drop it in front of her. She looks up at me with a scowl.

"Feel free to add something for yourself too," I tell her, turning around and going back to my desk.

She doesn't say anything but she gathers her things and leaves the office.

"Finally, a few moments to myself," I mumble, kicking my feet up on my desk and pulling out my phone to scroll through my messages.

I find one from Melinda: *I'm free tonight. Call me.*

I exit the message and go to the next from Ashley: *I'm single. Want to celebrate with me?*

I laugh and shake my head. The next is from Madison: *Hey, I'm back in town. This weekend only. Let's hook up!*

I clear all the messages and drop my phone onto my desk, wondering which one of them I should call tonight. Ashely is by far the hottest and dirtiest, but Madison is limited to this weekend. I think if I play this right, I can nail all three of them this weekend.

I pick up my phone and send Madison a quick text: *I get out of the office at 5. I'll pick you up at 7?* I hit send.

I reply to Ashely next: *I'm busy tonight. Raincheck for tomorrow?*

Finally, I text Melinda: *I'm swamped this weekend, babe. Will Sunday work?*

Happy with my quick thinking, I hit the button to turn the screen off and place it on my desk. The door to the office opens, and Val comes walking in with two bags. She holds one out, but before I can take it from her, she lets go, dropping it onto my desk. I frown at her, and that causes her to smile.

My phone starts going off.

Melinda: *Sunday will be perfect.*

Ashely: *Saturday night's fine with me.*

Madison: *See ya tonight.*

Val looks down at my phone and sees the three messages from three different women. She scrunches up her nose and makes this *ugh* noise before turning around and sitting at her desk to eat.

She doesn't say anything, and I don't either. I open my bag and pull out my food. I open my burger and take a big bite. I got way too wasted last night and skipped breakfast today. I need to put some food in my stomach to absorb some of that acid that's been making me sick all day. At first, everything is fine, but then the taste of mayo hits me. I gag and spit it out into the trash.

Val looks up at me with alarm.

"I wrote *no mayo*," I state flatly.

She shrugs. "Well, maybe if you didn't have the penmanship of a stressed-out doctor, I would've been able to read that."

"What else could it possibly say?" I ask, tossing the burger into the trash.

"I thought it said no Mayo—like Cinco de Mayo. I looked at the board and saw they didn't even have a Cinco de Mayo burger." She rolls her eyes.

I shake my head and bring my hands to my head, rubbing my temples. "I swear, you were put on this planet to give me a brain aneurism." I grab my jacket and leave the office. From now on, I'll be getting my own lunch.

The rest of the day passes in about the same fashion. I ask her to do something, she does it completely wrong on purpose, and then I get angry. I wish to God I could fire her. But I have a feeling she'd just run back to big brother's office on the top floor and complain about how I'm giving her demeaning jobs.

As five o'clock rolls around, I couldn't be happier. I run by the house, shower, shave, and dress for my date. I'm pulling up to her hotel at seven on the dot. I pull out my phone and send her a quick text, telling her I'm outside, and drop my phone into my lap. While I'm waiting, it rings, and I answer.

"Hello?"

"Hey, man," Bennet says. "How'd it go today?"

I scoff. "How do you think it went today?"

He lets out a nervous laugh. "Well, I just wanted to call and say thanks. I know she can be hard to handle, but she needs this job. I figured if you could make it past the first day, she would be safe."

My eyes roll on their own. I want to tell him that I'm done. I want to say fuck it and she's fired, but something inside of me stops the words before they can leave my lips. "No problem," I say instead.

"I'll let ya get back to whatever you were doing. But, Callan, I'm serious. Thanks. I don't know what else to do with her."

I laugh. "Now that I believe. See ya later." I hang up the phone just as Madison opens the door and slides inside. Looking over at her gets me excited. Her long, blonde hair is straight, hanging to her ass. She's wearing a short skirt and her top ends above her belly button, and it doesn't even start until half her tits are hanging out.

"Hey, babe," she says, leaning over and giving me a kiss while her hand cups my groin.

I smile as she pulls away. "Are you ready for an adventure?" I ask, shifting into drive.

"Always."

We make it to the club, and it's already in full swing. We're shown to the VIP area, and we sit at the bar, looking over the menu. She sips a fruity cocktail, and I opt for some Jameson, straight up.

While I'm reading over the menu, my hand is traveling up and down her thigh. Every time I get to the top, she opens her legs wider, hoping I move in. But I feel playful tonight. I feel like a chase. If all I wanted was a quick fuck, I could've gone up to her hotel room and been out in ten minutes. There would be no point to even taking her out. No, tonight I feel like flirting, driving her wild just to drive myself crazy. Maybe I'll even look to add someone to our little arrangement. I know she won't object. I've done many freaky things with this girl. I know a threesome with a random stranger isn't off the table.

She sucks down her drink at lightning speed, and she doesn't hesitate to order another. We both grab another round, then move to the center of the floor to dance while we wait for our food. She wraps her arms around my neck and pulls me closer, so close I can tell the drink she had was watermelon flavored and I haven't even kissed her yet. Her brown eyes look up, locking on mine, and she wets her bottom lip.

"What are we doing here, Callan?"

I shrug as I place one hand on her hip and begin grinding against her. "What do you mean?"

She smiles and looks at me from beneath her lashes like she's playing shy—something she's not. "We don't do this. We meet up, fuck, and go our separate ways. You know I'm not looking to settle down," she says around a smile.

I laugh loudly. "You're not the only one *not* looking to settle down. Why don't you look around the club and find someone you want to invite home with us?"

Her smile widens. "Okay," she whispers, pulling away and leaving the VIP section.

With her gone, I go back to the bar and sit down. Jimmy, the bartender, pours me another drink and shakes his head with a laugh. "I don't know how you do it, man."

I smirk. "Do what?"

"End up with all these different hotties every night."

I throw my drink back and set it down. Again, he refills it. "If you have enough money, or make it look like you do, you can get away with anything," I tell him, tipping my glass in his direction.

3

VALERIE

After work, I feel dead. It's like all the energy has been sucked from my body, and all because I had to hold myself back from telling Callan off all day. My muscles are tensed, making my back and neck sore and stiff. My head is pounding, and my eyes hurt from staring at a computer screen all day. This is definitely different than working in the art gallery.

I ride home with Bennet and Maddie, but as soon as we get to the house, I change into my own clothes and get behind the wheel to drive back to Mom's. When I walk in, she looks up with a smile. I think she likes having me live with her. She's been lonely since Dad passed.

"How was the first day?" she asks.

I collapse on the couch at her side and lay my head in her lap. "I hate it, Mom."

She laughs but starts combing through my hair with her fingers, something she's done since I was a child. It always soothes me. "Just hang in there. It will get better."

I sit up and look at her. "Remember how Callan and I bickered when we were kids?"

She laughs. "Boy, do I. There were days when I was ready to pull my hair out. I think you two are the reason I have so much gray," she teases.

My eyes stretch wide. "Well, it's only gotten worse. Except now we're adults, and there are no other adults around to tell us to shut up, so we just keep going and going." I roll my eyes.

She shakes her head. "Now, Valerie. You just have to remember that Callan is your boss. You can't talk to your boss that way. You, missy, are going to have to learn to bite your tongue."

I groan. "I know I've always been adamant about taking care of myself, but can you just support me for the rest of my life, so I never have to work again?" I ask, only half teasing.

She shakes her head. "Absolutely not. You know your father's feelings on this subject. I'm not going to disregard his wishes just because he isn't around to speak up anymore."

I stand. "Fine," I mumble, walking downstairs to my section of the house.

The one thing about this new, smaller house that I love is the way it's set up. Upstairs, which is ground level, is the living room, dining room, kitchen, two bedrooms, and a bathroom. But the downstairs has a full bathroom, three more bedrooms, and a living room section. I basically have my own house down here.

I strip out of my clothes from yesterday and step into the shower. I take an extra-long, extra-hot shower to help me forget my horrible day, then get out to pull on my pajamas. I think to myself how boring I must be to be in my pajamas at six on a Friday night, but I quickly forget as I toss myself onto the couch and turn on the TV.

I feel myself drifting in and out of sleep when my phone rings from beside me. I pull it to my ear.

"Hello?" I answer, sleep evident in my voice.

"Hey, what's going on?" Krista asks.

"Sleeping," I mumble.

"Sleeping? It's Friday night!"

I groan. "I know, but I've had a shit day."

"Bitch, get yo ass up! It's time to party!"

"But I don't wanna," I pout.

"Valerie Anne Windsor, get your ass up. Fix that face and put on something sexy. I'm on my way to get you." She hangs up without another word.

I drop the phone on the couch beside me and kick my feet, having a little fit. When the urge to cry wears off, I take a deep breath and push myself up, heading for my closet.

I find a red skin-tight dress and pull it on, pairing it with a pair of red fuck-me heels. The top is low cut, showing plenty of cleavage, and the skirt ends high on my thigh. I add some flashy earrings and bracelets before heading to the bathroom to do my hair and makeup. I quickly run the flat iron through my hair and leave it hanging around me. I paint my face, darkening my eyes and brightening my lips.

I'm putting a few things into my clutch when Krista walks down the stairs. She smiles wide when she sees me. "That's my girl," she says, eyes moving up and down my body in approval. "Are you ready for the night of your life?"

I laugh. "And what about tonight will make me think it's the night of my life?"

"I got Dillan, Decon, and Brian meeting us there. You get first pick," she tells me, shooting me a wink.

I roll my eyes. "We need to meet new boys," I tell her, closing my clutch and turning in her direction. "But I think Decon will be mine tonight."

She nods. "Nice choice."

———

WE'RE WALKING into the club about an hour later. It's already in full swing. The bar is crowded, the dance floor is full, and the tables are scarce. We both grab a drink before walking around the club, looking for a place to sit. We cross the dance floor, and the three guys are sitting in a corner booth, waving us down.

"Krista, Val, over here," Brian says, standing up in the booth until we walk over. Brian stands so I can slide in next to Decon.

Decon and I have been playing this *will they, won't they* game for months now. We flirt, dance, sometimes kiss, but we never end up going all the way for one reason or another. Maybe because it's more fun teasing one another.

"Hi, beautiful," Decon says, leaning in a pressing a kiss to my shoulder.

I smile from his lips tickling my skin. "Hey, where you been lately?"

"Oh, you know. Here and there," he says. "How about you?"

"I got a new job," I confess. "I sold out for a 401K and a tiny desk in the corner."

"That blows. Why don't we go dance off some of that steam?" He flashes me his sexy grin and pushes his dark hair out of his face.

I lift my drink and throw it back. "Sounds like a plan. Let's see if that rock-hard body of yours can make me forgot about my shitty day." He takes my hand in his and pulls me from the booth to the center of the dance floor.

I wrap my arms around his neck and pull myself closer. He places one hand on my hip while the other hangs casually at his side. Together, we move against one another. Our eyes lock, and he wets his bottom lip. Sweat is already beading up on his skin, and I feel him grow hard against me.

"How long we going to do this?" he asks, and I know exactly what he's referring to.

I shrug one shoulder and give him a teasing smile as I release him and spin around, pressing my ass to his crotch. He lets out a low grunt and grinds against me harder. His hands are now on my hips, moving up and down, working my dress up further and further with each lap. The song ends, and I step away.

"I'm going to get a drink," I whisper in his ear before walking away, leaving him wanting more.

That's usually my thing: always leave them wanting more. I smile to myself as I shake my ass a little more than necessary, just because I know he's watching.

When I get to the bar, I order my vodka cranberry to take back to the table but add on a shot of Patron while I wait for my drink to get mixed.

I feel someone bump against my shoulder. I look over, expecting to see Decon, but to my surprise, it's Callan.

"What are you doing here? Aren't you out past your bedtime?" he teases.

My smile immediately drops. "I didn't know they let dogs in here." I look around like I'm searching for a warning sign.

He mocks laughter, but I catch a glimpse of him through the corner of my eye. He looks me up and down slowly.

"Your mama let you out of the house dressed like that?" he asks, lifting his glass to his lips. "If you ask me, leaving the house like that is just asking for trouble."

That statement alone makes me want to walk away. "Excuse me, but the way I dress is none of your concern."

He seems taken aback.

I pick up my shot glass and throw it back. I toss some cash onto the bar, then grab my drink and walk away, feeling annoyed and irritated.

"There she is," Krista says as I walk back to the table.

"Here I am," I mumble, still overwhelmed with anger from running into Callan.

"What crawled up your ass?" she asks, moving out of my way so I can slide back into the booth.

"I just ran into Callan."

"Ugh, why do you let him bother you so much?"

I shrug and take a drink.

Decon wraps his arm around my shoulders, pulling me closer. "Forget about him and focus on me, Val. We have some catching up to do."

I force a smile onto my face. I really need to shake off this bad mood. Maybe tonight is the night I finally go all the way with Decon. God knows I could use it.

We sit back in the booth, talking, drinking, and laughing for several hours. Eventually, I forget all about Callan and find myself having fun. It's been a while since I was able to do something like this. Back when I was working at the gallery and was only making money when I sold one of my pieces, I didn't have the money to go out and do anything extra. But since I've been living with my mom, I've got a little in the bank, not to mention the good paychecks should hit next week. I think I deserve a night out, and I'm going to have a good time even if I have to force it.

Krista and Brian end up on the dance floor, and Dillan wanders off, trying to find him a piece for the night. Decon goes to get us both a fresh drink, and then we're left all alone in the dark corner booth. His fingers gently sweep up and down my thigh, and when I turn to face him, he catches my lips with his own. His lips are so plump and soft, they feel as if they cradle my own. His strong hand comes up to cup my cheek, holding me to him while he deepens our kiss. My hand seems to raise on its own, wrapping itself around his neck, wanting the kiss as much as he does. The alcohol seems to take over my body. Everything feels so good, euphoric even. I close my eyes and see the flashing colored lights from the club dancing behind my eyelids.

The longer we kiss, the more serious it gets. His hands are squeezing my breasts while his lips travel down my jaw and neck. Under the table, I find his hard cock, and I move my hand back and forth across his length.

"Let's take this outside," he whispers.

I pull back, look into his dark eyes, and nod. "Okay," I agree, feeling a little dizzy, but I tell myself it's just from the alcohol. I haven't been drunk like this in quite a while.

He stands and holds out his hand. I take it, and he leads me from the booth to the door, where we exit the building. His hands are on my shoulders from behind me, guiding me and keeping me upright.

Rounding the corner, there's a dark alley. It's dirty and dingy, and suddenly I'm confused as to why we're even out here. He pulls me against his strong chest and walks me backward until my back is against the cold brick building. His mouth finds mine and his tongue demands entrance.

My head is swirling. I feel confused and weak, like I'm unable to stop what's happening, but at the same time, enjoying the way his touches and kisses feel. He picks me up by my ass, and I squeal as my legs wrap around his hips. With me pinned between him and the wall, his hands fall between us, his fingers sliding into the side of my panties. My head lulls to the side, and all I can see is black, with a little light from the street peeking into the dark tunnel we're in. When his bare hand brushes against my sex, something inside of me snaps. It's only now I realize what's about to happen, and while I'm not totally against sleeping with him, I also don't want it in the dingy alley.

I push against his chest, wanting to be put back on my feet, but his hands on me tighten, and I can't get away from his kisses.

"Decon, stop," I say against his lips that are still moving quickly against mine.

I hear his zipper get pulled down, and a sudden rush of panic overwhelms me. I said stop, and he's not stopping. If I don't allow this, he will take what he wants.

"Owe," I cry out loud when he rips my panties from my body.

But he doesn't stop. Then a figure of a man steps into the alley.

"Hey!" he screams, causing us both to freeze and look his way.

4

CALLAN

I'm walking through the club when I see Val's little girlfriend. In all the years I've known them, they're always together. But now, she's grinding against some guy on the dance floor, and Val is nowhere to be found. I know that if she kept up drinking the way she was, she's beyond trashed right now.

I pull her friend, whose name I can't remember, off to the side. "Where's Val?" I ask loudly, above the music.

"She's in the booth over there with Decon. Hopefully getting laid by now." She smiles before rushing back to the guy she's with.

I shake my head, anger surging through my body. I swear, if I find her getting fucked in a club, I'm going to whip her ass and then tell her brother so he can ground her or some shit. I head back in the direction I was pointed to. The booth is empty.

"Fuck," I mumble, turning around. I walk through the club, and when I come back empty-handed, I walk outside.

The street is quiet, all but the busy traffic. I hear a woman yell, and I follow the sound around the corner. In the darkness, I can see two people against the building, and I immediately know it's her.

"Hey!" I yell, causing them both to freeze.

I start walking down the dark alley.

"What the fuck do you want?" a guy yells as I draw closer.

"Valerie, let's go," I demand.

"Hey, dickwad. I don't think she gives a shit what you have to say." He sets her down and fastens his belt while she stumbles forward, trying to right her dress. "Why don't you run along so we can get back to doing what we were doing before you interrupted," he says, walking closer.

Valerie pisses me off more than I can explain, but I know Bennet would kick my ass if I left her drunk in a dark alley to get treated like a hooker.

I don't say anything as we both walk closer to one another, but the second he's within reach, I swing, landing a solid hit to his jaw. It stuns him for a second, but then he jumps toward me, trying to take me to the ground, and I spin around, throwing my elbow down on his spine. He calls out in pain as he crumbles to the ground. I pull my foot back and land a kick to his stomach, making sure he stays down.

I hold out my hand. "Now, Valerie." I look into her eyes and can see she's fucked up. It's almost like she doesn't even recognize me. Her eyes are wide with fear as she shakes her head and takes a step back. Her ankle rolls in those shoes and she tumbles back on her ass.

"Damnit, Valerie. Get up and come with me now or I'll pick your ass up and carry you."

"Fuck you, Callan. You don't get to tell me what to do." She sounds like a spoiled teenager right now. So she does know who I am.

I let out a deep breath, then bend down and haul her ass over my shoulder. She smacks my back. "Put me down, Callan!" she yells as I walk down the alley with her, but I don't. No fucking way I'm leaving her drunk ass alone in this alley with that guy.

I walk her out of the alley and to my car before I set her on her feet. The second she's standing on her own, she stumbles and topples over. Luckily for her, I reach out and catch her.

"Whoa, you alright?" I ask, steadying her.

She smacks my hand away as she leans against my car. Her face is suddenly void of emotion.

"Val, are you okay? Did he slip you something?" I ask, but it seems like her eyes aren't focusing on me.

Suddenly, she bends over and empties her stomach all over my shoes.

"Goddamn it!" I yell, opening the car door for her. I place my hands on her shoulders and gently move her over to the seat. She sits down, hanging her head between her legs while she finishes emptying her stomach. Finally, she leans back, and I pick up her feet, putting them into the floorboard. I close the door between us and kick the fucking tire.

So much for my threesome I had lined up.

I walk around the car, sit in the driver's seat, and then look at my shoes that are covered in vomit. Deciding to say fuck it, I kick them off and leave them laying in the street, driving home in my bare feet.

Valerie sleeps the entire way, and she doesn't stir when I try waking her. I end up having to carry her into the house. I cradle her against my chest and carry her upstairs. Her head rolls from one side to the other, but she doesn't wake up.

I lay her in the bed in the guest room and remove her shoes. I can't imagine keeping my feet squeezed into such impossible shoes all night. When I step back and look down at her, I see the front of her dress covered in vomit.

"What the fuck, Val?" I whisper, shaking my head.

I quickly grab a large t-shirt out of my room and walk back to get her changed. I roll her to the side and unzip her dress. I've only got the zipper down a couple of inches, but already I can tell she isn't wearing a bra. I close my eyes and take a deep breath.

I step back, wondering how in the hell I can get her changed without seeming like a creep that's stripping the drunk girl. In the end, I pull her arms out of the sleeves of the dress but leave the material up over her chest before pulling on the t-shirt. After working the shirt down over her body, I pull the dress out from underneath. Finally, I pull the blankets up her body. As I turn to leave, I hear her gag in her sleep, and I rush back to roll her onto her side. It seems she has nothing left to kick out of her body, but she's still dry heaving.

Once I'm sure she's done and back asleep, I leave the room. I go into my room next door and strip down to my boxers. Then decide I should bring in a trash can and a bottle of water. I run down to the kitchen and get both before taking them back to her room. Finally, I'm able to lay down, but I can't fall asleep. I'm too worried. What if she gets sick in her sleep and chokes? God, I'd never hear the end of it from Bennet.

"Motherfucker, goddamn, son of a bitch," I curse as I nearly stomp back to her room. I get in the bed beside her, so I'll wake if something happens. I scoot to the furthest edge of the bed, not wanting any confusion in the morning.

———

I HEAR A GASP, and my eyes pop open. My arm is under her neck, her knee against my morning wood.

"What the fuck, Callan?" she squeals, pulling away from me.

I shoot up into an upright position, darting out of bed. Her eyes take me in, in nothing but my boxers.

Her eyes grow wide as she shakes her head. "No. No, no, no, no." She looks down to find herself in nothing but a t-shirt.

Suddenly, I'm panicked. My head is shaking, and my hands are waving back and forth. "No, Val. Nothing happened. Fuck no," I tell her.

She freezes. "No-nothing happened?" she asks, eyes filled with fear.

I fall onto the bed in a sitting position. "If you call getting slipped the date rape drug and being taken out to an alley nothing, then yeah. Nothing happened."

"What?" she asks, confused.

"What do you remember about last night?" I ask her.

She thinks for a moment. "I remember going to the club, seeing you, hanging out with Decon. We got a little too close in the club, and I remember going outside. But that's it."

"You don't remember me stopping you from getting fucked in

an alley?"

Her head falls forward, and her shoulders slump. "No," she admits.

"You don't remember puking all over your dress and my shoes?"

She shakes her head. "How did I get in this shirt, anyway?"

"I put it on you."

"You what?" she yells, pulling the blanket up over her shoulders.

"Don't worry. I didn't see anything. I was a complete gentleman."

She snorts. "I find that hard to believe."

"Me too, but I was. I swear. I know we both hate each other, but you're my best friend's sister. I don't want to see you hurt, okay?"

She offers up a small smile and nods. "God, my fucking head hurts." She massages her temples.

"Yeah, I've heard drugs do that to you. You should probably take a test to see what exactly you were spiked with."

She lays back down. "Do you care if I just sleep it off a little while?"

I stand. "Sure. I'll call Bennet and let him know that you're here." I head for the door.

She shoots up. "No, Callan, please don't tell him."

"What am I supposed to tell him then? How can I explain you staying the night? I'd rather have him thinking that I rescued you than slept with you."

One of her brows lifts. "Okay, just, let him know that I'm fine. I'll deal with him later."

She lays back down, and I leave the room, ready to shower and maybe catch another couple hours of sleep.

"Hello?" Bennet answers.

"Hey, man," I say, pouring a glass of water.

"What's up?"

"I just wanted to give you a call and fill you in on the recent turn of events."

"Oh yeah?"

"Yeah, I, ugh…went to the club last night and ran into your sister. She was with some asshole, and I think he slipped her something. I caught him in the alley with her, and she doesn't remember any of it. She got really sick, so I brought her back to my place. She's fine, but she's not feeling well, and she's sleeping it off. I just didn't want you or your mom to worry."

He lets out a deep breath. "Fuck," he breathes out. "Thanks, Cal. I owe you one."

"Yeah, you do," I agree. "A new pair of shoes, preferably like the ones she puked on."

"Seriously, I don't know what my mom would do if anything happened to her. She's the baby, you know?"

I nod. "Yeah, well, she's fine. You know she drives me crazy, but I'd never turn my back on her, or you."

"Should I come get her?" he asks.

"Nah, she's asleep. Just let her sleep it off, and I'll take her home later."

"Alright. Thanks again."

"No problem," I say, hanging up the phone and tossing it onto the empty bed.

———

I TAKE A NAP, shower, dress, and head downstairs to try and find a late lunch. I make a big sandwich with ham, turkey, cheese, lettuce, tomato, and mustard. I grab a bag of chips and a jar of pickles before heading back to the dining room table. I've just taken a bite out of the sandwich when Val walks into the room. She looks rough as hell. Her hair is a tangled mess, she has dark circles under her eyes, and her skin is pale. She collapses into the chair next to me.

"Feeling okay?" I ask, picking up half the sandwich and sliding the plate her way.

She looks at the plate and then at me. "Why are you being so nice to me?"

I shrug and take a bite of my sandwich. "I figure you've had enough shit to deal with, and even more coming your way with your mom and brother."

She picks up the other half of my sandwich and takes a bite. Her eyes close as her head leans back. "This is so good."

"Are you sure you're feeling good? It's just a sandwich, nothing special."

"My head is still pounding. And I feel weird. It's like, I keep trying to remember something that I never knew to begin with."

"I don't think you want to remember anything from last night."

"That bad? I didn't flash anyone, right?"

I laugh and shrug. "No idea what you did before I found you in that alley. Who the fuck was the guy you were with? He needs to be straightened out."

"It's this guy I met working at the art gallery. His name is Decon James. I can't believe he'd drug me. We've known one another for almost a year."

"And by known, you mean…?"

She moves her head from side to side. "We make-out, flirt, hang. We've never slept together."

"I'd say Decon figured if he couldn't seal the deal himself, he was going to bring backup."

"I feel so stupid," she breathes out. "And embarrassed."

"It's nothing to be embarrassed about. You didn't take the drug willingly, did you?"

She frowns at me. "No way. I don't do drugs. Never have."

I nod. "That's all I needed to know." Already, I'm picturing tracking this guy down and beating his fucking brains out for pulling that shit. And it's not just over Val. It's the fact that he's probably done this to many girls and has gotten away with it. I can't wait to run into Decon James again. I can't help the smile that appears on my face.

5

VALERIE

Looking at Callan right now, something feels different. He no longer pisses me off just by looking at me. His voice is suddenly tolerable. He doesn't even appear the same. That smug, cocky look I usually see when I glance at him is gone. Maybe last night was what we needed to be able to work together. Maybe it's the start of our friendship.

We both sit quietly and eat the sandwich and chips. He reaches over and pops the top of the pickle jar. He takes one and shoves the whole spear into his mouth before sliding it to me. I smile, take one, and do the same. His eyes double in size and the corners of his mouth turn up.

I slide the jar back to him, and he repeats the process, and so do I. We do this back and forth until the entire jar is gone.

"Thanks for lunch," I say, standing. "You mind if I shower? I don't want to give my mom a heart attack walking back in the house looking like this."

He lets out a laugh. "No, go ahead. I'll dig you out some clothes and leave them on the bed for you. I highly doubt you will ever want to wear that dress again."

My face scrunches up, and I feel the heat suddenly radiating off it.

He chuckles. "Are you embarrassed?"

"Well, yeah! Wouldn't you be?" I ask as he stands and picks up the plate to put it away.

He places his hand on my bicep. "At this point, I think you should just be thankful to be alive." He smiles kindly and walks away, leaving me staring after him.

On my walk up the stairs, I think about the way he's suddenly acting toward me. It's nice and all, but it's weird, and it makes me leery of when he's going to go back to the old Callan, the one that lived to torture me. I brush the thoughts off, telling myself that he'll probably rear his ugly head first thing Monday morning to welcome me back.

A part of me wonders if he's worried about me. He seems that way. Like he's scared to push my buttons in fear I may break open at any moment. I guess what I've gone through is a traumatic experience, but truthfully, I don't remember any of it. I'm just glad Callan was there to save me. I don't know what I would've done had I woken up in that alley alone this morning, missing my clothing. Just thinking of it makes me shudder.

I take a long hot shower, and when I get out, I find fresh clothing for me folded up on the bed. I pull on the pair of baggy basketball shorts and the t-shirt. Then I begin to look around for my clutch. Callan taps on the door before opening it.

"Are you ready for a ride home?"

I spin around. "Where's my purse?"

His mouth opens, but no words come out.

"Fuck, I lost my purse?"

"I...I don't...I didn't see a purse." He walks deeper into the room, eyes full of regret.

"Can you take me back to the club? Maybe someone turned it in?"

He nods. "Yeah, okay."

We load up into his car, and he parks out front. I look over at him and he looks over at me.

"Are you going to run in?" he asks.

"Looking like this?" I motion down my body. "I don't even have shoes."

He lets out a deep breath. "Okay," he says, climbing out and walking into the building.

I sit waiting, my legs bouncing the whole time. Finally, he walks out, and I catch a glimpse of my red clutch under his arm. It feels like my heart starts beating again.

He slides into the car and passes it over. I take it and immediately start looking through it.

The only things inside are my I.D. and lipstick. "Fuck," I breathe out, slumping into my seat.

"What?" he asks, pulling back out into traffic.

"My phone and money are gone," I tell him.

"How much money?"

I wave it off. "Not enough to worry about. Luckily, I didn't bring my entire wallet that has my debit card and credit cards. But my phone? I need my phone."

"I'll just swing in someplace. We'll get you another one, and you can just download everything from the cloud."

"I can't afford a new phone," I cry out. "I can't even afford toilet paper."

He laughs. "Don't worry about it, Val. We'll write it off for work. I like my assistants to have phones so I can bug them anytime I need to."

I look over at him. "Thank you, Callan."

He waves his hand through the air. "It's nothing. Thank your brother if you're going to thank anyone." He laughs.

Unfortunately, I have to go into the phone store so I can authorize everything, but an hour later, we're back in the car with my new phone—a phone much nicer than the one I had. While everything downloads, I look over at him.

"So, does everything go back to normal on Monday?"

He glances at me from the corner of his eye. "What do you mean?"

"I mean, when I go into the office on Monday, will I see this Callan or the Callan I've known my whole life?"

He laughs. "I guess you'll have to wait and see."

I roll my eyes. "Too bad I didn't get to know this side of you first. We probably could've saved each other a lot of headaches."

He laughs. "Yeah, but it's been fun. You can't deny that. Even when you're pissing me off, I still like to hear the shit that comes out of your mouth. You always surprise me." He looks over at me, and the smile he's wearing is genuine. It's not the cocky smile he usually has. It's not the flirty smiles he uses with women. This is the kind of smile I've only ever seen him have when he's enjoying talking with friends, like my brother. It's nice to be on the receiving end for once.

He pulls into my mom's driveway and shifts into park as he looks over at me.

"Thank you," I tell him, feeling that the words aren't enough.

"Stop saying that, Val. I didn't do anything special."

I nod. "You did, though. I could be laying in a hospital bed right now if it weren't for you."

His hand lands on my bare knee, and he squeezes it playfully. "Let's not think about what could've happened. Let's just be thankful things went the way they did."

I nod, agreeing with him, but I can't ignore the way my heart started pounding when his hand touched my skin. Unsure of what's going on, I reach for the handle and open the door. His hand moves back to the steering wheel. He didn't seem to notice the gesture the way I did, so I don't mention it.

"See you on Monday," I say, stepping out and closing the door behind me. On my walk to the door, I glance over my shoulder, expecting him to be backing down the drive, but he's still in the same place, watching to make sure I get inside. Just before I step through the front door, I wave and so does he.

I close the door behind me and lean my back against it. For some reason, I'm breathless. My heart is racing, and my stomach muscles are tightened. I tell myself that I need to relax; it's probably just the after-effects of whatever I ingested last night.

"Hey, sweet pea," Mom says, walking into the living room with a cup of tea. Then she fully takes me in, and her lips part as fear fills her eyes. "What happened to you? Are you okay?"

I nod and stand upright. "I got a little sick last night, but Callan found me and took me back to his place. He stayed by my side all night to make sure I was okay."

She smiles. "See, I've always told you that he was a nice boy. But why did you get sick? I hope you weren't out binge drinking like all these kids do nowadays."

I shake my head as I start walking toward the stairs. "I think it was something I ate. I'm never eating sushi again."

When I get downstairs, I collapse onto the couch and turn on the TV while I kick back and try relaxing. My head is still pounding. I think the only thing that will make it ease up is time. My phone rings and I answer it.

"Hello?"

"Hey, where have you been? I've been calling you since last night," Krista says.

I don't even know how to answer that. "Did you not notice me missing?" I ask.

"I mean...not for a while. I was dancing with Brian. Decon went MIA too, so I just thought you guys were finally following through. You've had like, what, a year of foreplay?"

I shake my head. "He drugged me, Kris. I don't remember anything, but luckily Callan showed up and saved me from getting raped in the alley."

"Don't be dramatic, Val. We've known Decon for a year. He wouldn't do something like that."

"Callan wouldn't lie about that, Kris. You need to be careful around him. Promise me you won't go hang out with those guys anymore."

"I just left Brian's house, and everything is fine."

"Promise me you won't be alone with Decon, Kris. I'm serious. Things could've ended up a lot worse for me. I don't want anything to happen to you."

"Alright, I promise. Are you okay?"

"I lost my phone, ruined my shoes and dress, but yeah, I'm fine. I really owe Callan."

"God, I feel so bad. I honestly didn't think Decon would do something like that," she says, guilt dripping from her words.

"Me neither," I agree with a nod.

————

THE REST of the weekend is spent laying on the couch, hanging out with my mom, and eating way too much food. Monday morning rolls around, and I'm almost looking forward to getting back into the office, and I don't know why. I guess a part of me wants to see how Callan acts toward me. It feels like we finally broke the ice on our friendship this weekend, like we just needed one thing to bond over. Too bad that thing was me being taken advantage of.

I shower and dress in a black skirt, white shirt, and red heels. I leave my hair down but curl it to make it look a little nicer, and I add a small amount of makeup. When I walk into the office, Callan is already behind his desk. His head pops up, and he almost smiles, but then decides against it.

"There's a list on your desk of things I need done today," he says flatly, turning his attention back to his computer.

"Okay," I say, taking my seat. As I slide my purse beneath my desk, I look up and study him. It seems his easy-going attitude from this weekend has left his body. And in its place is the Callan that's spent all his time torturing me.

For the first half of the day, I sit at my desk, and he sits at his. We each do our jobs, and neither of us says a word. Around noon, he walks over and hands me a piece of paper with his lunch order. I grab my purse and head to the door. I glance down at the paper and see the same order from the other day.

"No mayo, right?" I ask, pausing, trying any way I can to get him to talk to me.

He looks up, offers a generic smile, and nods.

I leave without another word. I step into the elevator and bump into Maddie.

"Oh, Val. Bennet told me what happened. Are you okay?" she asks, latching onto my arm.

I nod. "I'm fine. I just..." I let my sentence drift off.

"What?" she asks.

"Well, it's just that after all that happened, Callan was really great. He was friendly, and it felt like we may be becoming friends. But now, he's downright refusing to acknowledge me."

Maddie offers up a small smile. "Don't take it personally, Val. Who knows what he's thinking? He's probably just freaked out in the sudden change in your relationship."

"I guess," I say, stepping off the elevator with her following behind me.

"Just give it some time. He'll either go back to how he was before, or this new friendship will take over."

"Hopefully the latter," I say with a laugh.

6

CALLAN

When I reach out and touch her leg—something I mean to be completely innocent—my heart halts and leaps to my throat. My face feels hot and a little tingly. I quickly think I'm having a heart attack, but then she steps into the house, and my whole body calms down. What the fuck was that? I've never in my life felt something so strongly. It couldn't be because of her, could it?

I back down the driveway, thoughts racing a mile a minute. Do I have feelings for Valerie? That thought alone makes me want to laugh. I can't have feelings for Valerie. She's my best friend's little sister. He'd fucking kill me if I laid a hand on her. And, hello, it's fucking Valerie. The girl I can't fucking stand.

But I saw her in a totally different light. For once, she wasn't the person trying to fuck up my life; she was the person about to have her life fucked up. She was taken advantage of and used. And that's not okay with me. But what was that, that spark I felt when we touched? Am I attracted to her at all? She's beautiful, I suppose. She's tall, thin, and has gorgeous features. I guess I've never looked at her like that. But if I think about it, she is quite striking.

Fuck, I need more sleep.

I drive back home and crash into bed, instantly drifting off to sleep, but behind my lids, I see her. I see her innocent eyes, her big smile, her soft lips. I can see myself moving closer to her, kissing her, touching her. I can hear her soft moans and gasps. I can smell her, taste her. And it's all heavenly.

My eyes pop open, and my heart is racing. What the fuck is going on with me? I take a deep breath to clear my head. It's obviously just a little mix up in my brain. This weekend, I saw a different side of her, not to mention I didn't seal the deal with my date. I'm probably just horny, and I've spent more time with her than I ever have. Clearly, I don't have feelings for my best friend's sister. I can't. I won't.

My phone chimes from beside me, and I lift it to read the message. It's from Ashley: *I'm looking forward to tonight.*

Fuck, I forgot about that. But I guess I'll be able to bang these feelings and urges out of me.

Be there soon, I reply.

I FORCE myself to get up and get in the car. I don't feel like meeting up with a girl and having casual sex. I'd much rather sit at home and relax while trying to figure this thing out, but that's not what I do. I live life; I have fun. Deep down, I'm hoping that tonight will erase these confusing feelings I'm having about Val.

———

I SLIDE INTO ASHELY, and she feels amazing wrapped around me. I close my eyes, and in my head, it's not Ashley I'm with: it's Val. I can see the way her plump lips part with her heavy breathing. I can hear her calling out my name. I can feel my heart pounding like it will jump from my chest at any moment. And when I finish, it feels like nothing I've ever felt before. It's like coming for the first time.

When I get back home, all I can think about is Valerie. The whole point of tonight was to get my rocks off in hopes of getting rid of this attraction I'm suddenly feeling to her but picturing myself fucking her instead of the girl I was with, it only made the attraction take hold that much more.

I want Valerie in my bed. I want to know what it would be like to slide into her. I want to know how she tastes, how soft her skin is against my lips. I want to fucking own her.

"Fuck my life," I mumble, laying my head back as I look at the white ceiling above my bed.

———

WHEN SHE LEAVES to get my lunch, I feel like I can breathe again. I know she's noticed a difference in the way I'm acting, but I honestly have no idea how to be around her anymore. I fucking want her, and I can't have her. Even if she'd allow it, I never could because I know Bennet wouldn't stand for it. I'd probably lose my job. I know I'd lose my best friend. I can't spend eight hours a day with her in this secluded office. If I didn't have to look up and see her, if I didn't have to smell her sweet perfume drifting my way, I could keep my distance.

While she's gone, I pick up the phone and call the maintenance guy. He walks in moments later.

"You said you needed help, Mr. Gregory?"

"Yes," I stand. "I do." I walk to the center of the room. "I need help moving this desk out of my office."

"Into the hallway?" he asks, confused.

"Exactly," I reply. "Now, come on."

He takes one end of the desk, and I take the other. We move it out of the office and into a rather large seating area just outside my door.

I stand back and look at our handy work. That'll do.

I quickly rush inside and get her chair, putting it with her desk. The moment I sit behind my desk, she comes walking in, looking pissed as hell.

"What the fuck, Callan?" she asks, dropping my lunch onto my desk and motioning toward her desk that's no longer in the office.

I take a deep breath. "After last week, I thought it might be easier on both of us to have our breathing room. It's nothing personal."

She snaps her mouth closed, nods her head, and turns to leave without a word.

Wow, that went better than I thought.

When the maintenance man gets back from lunch, I have him set up our phones so I can page her at her desk for when I need something. This seems like a much better arrangement. Now, maybe I'll be able to get her off my mind and keep my damn hands to myself.

As I'm finishing up my lunch, Bennet walks into my office. "Callan, what the hell is that?" he asks, pointing toward the door.

I shrug. "It seemed like the better option." I can't tell him I'm fantasizing about fucking his little sister and this is the only way I can trust myself.

"I thought after this past weekend, you two would be getting along a little better. What did she do, anyway?"

"She didn't do anything," I confess. "I just think this is better. I have my office to myself, and you won't have to listen to her complain about me every day. Win-win."

He shakes his head and rolls his eyes. "Whatever, man. It's fine by me." He walks out without another word.

The workweek passes quickly, but not quickly enough. I guess Val decided that me moving her desk was a personal attack, and she won't even look my way. She'll answer any question I ask, and she'll do any task I give her, but friendly Val is gone. On the other hand, so is ornery Val. She doesn't joke or tease me. In fact, she goes out of her way to avoid me at all costs. The only problem is, every night when I'm alone or with another girl, she's the only fucking thing I can think about. Putting distance between us isn't working for me. In fact, it's only making me think of her more.

I try working my issues out on other women, but none of them can get the job done. I picture fucking her over and over, and each time, my release gets weaker and weaker. It gets to the point that I have issues getting hard altogether. I'm annoyed, angry, and wound tight. Even though I want to have sex and have it end well, my body won't cooperate.

It's Friday evening, and most of the staff have left for the day. It's only myself and Valerie left on this floor. I'm at my desk, and she's at hers, finishing up our work so we can leave for the weekend. She opens my door and walks in. It closes gently behind her. I watch her walk up to me with determination. She places a file folder in front of me.

"There. Can I go now?"

I nod once, not bothering to talk.

She turns on her heel, but before she can get to the door, she spins back around. "What the hell is your problem, Callan?"

My mouth drops open. "I don't have a problem, Val."

"Well, something is going on. I thought we were getting along well. Then the next thing I know, I'm kicked out of the office. What gives?"

I stand up and take a deep breath. "There's nothing wrong. I just thought this would work better for the two of us."

She shakes her head and takes a deep breath that causes her chest to rise. With her hands on her hips, she begins walking closer, and it makes me want to take a step back to keep our distance. I know if she gets close enough, I'll end up doing something I regret. This is Valerie. She isn't just some random woman that wants a good time. If I touch her, I might as well pack my bags and leave everything and everyone I know.

"Something is going on, Callan. Last Saturday, we were like old friends, talking and laughing. You were going out of your way to help me, and now you can hardly look me in the eye." She comes to a stop directly in front of me. I can smell her perfume. I can practically feel the heat leaving her body.

I look up, and our eyes lock. I can see anger and passion brewing behind them. She licks her bottom lip, wetting it, and her lips part. It gives me flashbacks to that first dream I had. I can feel myself starting to waver. I'm thinking things like: just one touch, one little kiss. I can blame it on being confused by our new friendship. I can completely dismiss it. I'm sure she wouldn't tell Bennet. I mean, it's just a kiss, practically nothing. Maybe it will be enough to get her out of my head. I mean, if I kiss her and feel nothing, this confusion will go away, right?

But what if it makes it worse? What if I kiss her and can't stop? What if it leads to other things? I need to get her away from me as quickly as possible.

"Damnit, Valerie. I was just being nice because you'd had a shitty night. I did what I had to do for my best friend's sister. Okay? It wasn't a bonding moment. It didn't mean anything to me. Stop reading into everything." I shake my head, getting angry at myself. "Why don't you just go home? We're done here." I pick up the file she dropped on my desk and turn my back to her, filing it away in the cabinet for Monday. I close the drawer, and a deep breath leaves me. When I turn around, my door is standing wide open, and she's nowhere in sight.

Part of me is happy because I managed to get her to leave without doing something I shouldn't. But another part of me is angry that I'm too scared to reach out and take something I want. This seems like a no-win situation for me.

As I'm leaving the office, I keep trying to think of ways to get her out of my head, but everything I've already tried doesn't seem to work. I need more space. That's the only thing that will work. I need to be rid of her once and for all.

Monday morning, I'm going to fire her. I don't care if I end up having to answer my own phone calls. At least I'll still have a job, and my best friend. The more time that passes, the better I'll feel until there is nothing left for her anyway.

Just knowing what Monday will bring makes me angry and puts me in a bad mood. Everything about me is tense and sore. My temper is through the roof, and I feel like I'll snap at the smallest of things.

When I get home, I pour a stiff drink and sit behind my desk, debating whether or not I should call Bennet and give him a heads up. I'm sure he'll ask me why I want to fire her. I'm going to need an actual answer. I mull it over and decide just to get it over with. After I talk to him, I'll call her and fire her. Then I won't even have to worry about seeing her on Monday. Maybe I'll feel better and be able to enjoy my weekend instead of dreading the coming week.

I grab my phone and call Bennet.

"Hello?" he answers.

"Hey, man. What's up?" I ask, taking a sip in hopes of being drunk before I tell him the reason for this call.

"Nothing much. I'm just in the garage, working on a car. What's up with you?"

I chew the inside of my cheek. "I want to talk about something. You care if I swing by?"

"No, not at all."

"Alright, see you soon." I hang up and gather my wallet, phone, and keys to leave.

I get to his place a little while later, and instead of going into the house, I go straight to the garage. When I walk in, his head is under the hood of the car and the music is so loud, I know he didn't hear me enter. I walk over and rasp my knuckles against the hood. He pops out quickly. At first, fear is in his eyes, but then he sees it's me and his face smooths while a smile takes over. He moves to turn down the music.

"You scared the shit out of me," he says around a laugh.

I lean against the car and cross my arms with a small smile.

"What's going on? I know something is bothering you. Is it Val?" he asks, moving to the cooler and grabbing two beers.

I take the drink I'm offered, open it, and take a sip. "I got to let her go," I confess, shaking my head and letting it hang.

"What? Why?" he asks, eyes wide and back stiff.

7

VALERIE

I'm sitting on the couch downstairs when the phone rings. I pick it up. "Hello?"

"What's up?" Krista asks.

I let out a long breath. "Nothing," I reply, wanting to say more but not sure how to.

"What's going on, Val?" she asks again.

"I've had a shitty week."

"No surprise there," she mumbles.

"No, it isn't like last week. Last week was fun compared to this week."

"How so?"

I hold up the remote and shut off the TV, so I have no distractions. "Last week, Callan and I were doing our usual thing. You know, pissing one another off on purpose. I hated it then, but looking back, I can see that's just our way. Like, it was our version of friendship, I guess. But then after last weekend, things changed. He took care of me even after I puked all over him. He slept next to me to make sure I didn't die. He drove me around and made me lunch. We talked, and everything was great. I thought it was a new start for us, like we were finally becoming real friends. It gave me hope for work. But then I went in on Monday, and he was cold. We didn't go back to how we were. Instead, he was going out of his way to ignore me. The only time he would talk to me is when he was telling me to do a job. I went and got our lunch on Monday, and when I came back, my desk was moved out into the hall. No explanation or anything. I don't know what I did wrong. I was so happy that we had seemed to put everything behind us and start fresh, and then the next thing I know, it's like he hates me so much now, he can't even bear to look at me."

I hear her take a deep breath. "Just seduce him and fuck him. I'm sure that's all he needs."

I shake my head, annoyed that she isn't taking this seriously. "I gotta go, Kris." I hang up before she can say anything else.

I call Maddie because she always knows what to say or do.

"Hello?" she answers.

"Hey, Mads. What are you guys up to tonight?" I ask, sitting up and crossing my legs beneath me.

"Not much of anything. Bennet is out in the garage, needing to finish up a car so he can have it delivered on time. I'm just sitting in the house, drinking some wine and reading a book."

"Mind if I come over or is that book too good to put down? I need some girl talk."

She giggles. "I already have a glass out for you."

Her words make me smile. "Okay, I'll be over soon."

I stand and slide my feet into a pair of flip flops. I grab my purse, phone, and keys, and head for the door.

When I pull in a little while later, the driveway is full, so I end up pulling my car into the yard. I walk to the front door, and she must have heard me pull in because she's opening it just as I'm preparing to knock.

She smiles. "I figured that was you."

"Thanks for letting me come over. I tried talking to Krista about this, but her only advice was to fuck him."

She laughs as she grabs the bottle of wine and two glasses and leads me out onto the back porch. "Are we having more Callan talk?"

I want to roll my eyes. Surely, she's sick of hearing about him already. "You know it."

We both sit in our deck chairs, and she pours two glasses, handing me one. "Okay, shoot."

And I do. I tell her everything I told Krista. When I finish, she looks out at the lawn, thinking everything over.

"So, what do you think?"

"I think things got complicated."

"Duh," I say. "But why?"

She takes a sip of her wine. "I honestly have no idea. My bet is that he found himself having different feelings for you and doesn't know how to handle them or how to react."

"Different feelings? Like what?"

"Like maybe spending that night together made him see you differently. Now, you're not his best friend's annoying little sister. You're a woman that he found things in common with. He's either confused by the sudden change in your relationship, or he's struggling with something."

I let my head fall back as a deep breath leaves my lips. "But what I am supposed to do? I mean, I don't even see him at work hardly. If he needs something, he will send a message to my computer, or he'll call my phone. He's gone out of his way not to have to deal with me."

"Just give it time? Let things calm down and do your job. Don't give him a reason to fire you. Sooner or later, he'll come around, I'm sure."

I nod and finish off my glass. My phone chimes from inside my purse and I pull it out. It's a text from Callan.

I'm really sorry to have to do this, but I don't think our arrangement is going to work out. I already told Bennet, and he's trying to find you another place in the company. I'm really sorry, Val.

My mouth drops open, and I gasp.

"What?" Maddie asks, jerking her head in my direction.

"He just fucking fired me. Over a text message!"

Her eyes widen, and her mouth drops open. "Does it say why?"

I shake my head. "Just that our arrangement isn't working, and Bennet is already trying to find me a new position."

"Bennet knows? I wonder why he didn't say anything?" she asks more to herself than anyone else.

Just then, we hear a car start up, and I stand to look around the corner of the house. It's Callan's car.

"Who is it?" Maddie asks, not moving from her chair.

"It's Callan. He's been in the garage with Bennet," I reply, looking toward the garage in time to see Bennet walking out, toward us.

He walks up the stairs like nothing's wrong. He goes into the house, grabs a beer, and walks back out holding it to his lips. Suddenly, he realizes that I and Maddie both are starting at him.

"What?" he asks, confused.

"What?" Maddie repeats, shaking her head and rubbing her temples.

"What the hell was that?" I motion toward Callan's car that's no longer in the driveway.

"Cal just came by to talk."

"He just fired me!" I yell.

He nods. "Yeah, I know. But don't worry, Val. We'll find you something else."

I shake my head. "Why did he fire me?"

"Oh," he says, trying to think something up. "Well, it's just not working out. He says that you don't respect him, that every time he gives you a job to do, you mess it up on purpose. He said you talk back and make fun of him. Not that he cares about it personally; it's just a very inappropriate work environment."

My mouth drops open. "That is completely untrue! Last week, yeah, we were both acting that way. But this week, I've barely said two words to him, and I do every task he gives me perfectly. There's something else going on." I cross my arms and lean against the railing.

"I'm sorry, Val," Bennet says, squeezing my arm as he walks back to the garage.

I look at Maddie. "This pisses me off so bad. I mean, last week, I wouldn't have cared to have been fired, but this week, I've done nothing to deserve it."

"Then demand a real answer," Maddie says.

I nod. "I'm going to. I'm going to make him talk to me, explain himself." I walk back toward my chair and grab my purse.

"Now? You're doing this now?" she asks.

I nod. "Yep, no time like the present," I say, walking down the steps and around the house toward my car. I get behind the wheel and start driving back toward the city. Traffic is heavy, and in a way, I'm thankful because it gives me time to sort through my thoughts. I'm way too angry to confront him right now. With my anger, my attitude will be high, and my attitude will only anger him. That's not the way to get my job back.

Do I want that job back?

I guess, if he has a good explanation for firing me, then I will let it go. But being fired for no reason is not okay. I demand to be treated with respect. Truthfully, I could probably hire a lawyer and sue the company for this. I wouldn't. I mean, it's my brother's company, but still. What he did is wrong on every level, and I'm not going to let him get away with it easily.

By the time I get to his house, I've cooled off some, but I'm still determined to get an answer out of him one way or another. I park the car in front of his house and climb out. I march up to the door and knock hard and loud. There's no way he can ignore me with the way I'm pounding.

The door flies open, and I can see the alarm on his face until he sees me standing there. "Val? What the hell?" he asks, breathing like he just sprinted to the door. "I thought someone was being chased by a murderer out here."

I push my way inside. "It's time we talked, Callan," I say, spinning around to confront him. "You cannot fire me. Do you hear me?"

He closes the door and holds up his hands, palms facing me. "Val, I'm sorry. I didn't want to do this."

"Then why are you doing it?" I yell, holding my arms out at my sides. "I thought we'd finally established a friendship between us.

Then suddenly, you're completely cold. It's like you hate the sight of me. Like you'd rather take the easy way out and fire me than to have to look at me for another second. What did I do to cause this?" I ask, feeling my body grow hot from anger.

He doesn't answer me. Instead, he starts walking deeper into the house without saying a word. He leaves me standing in the foyer alone, speechless. Finally, I follow after him, not sure if this is what he was wanting me to do. But I refuse to leave without an answer.

I walk into his home office and find him standing at his drink cart, sipping on some whiskey. I lean my shoulder against the door jam and cross my arms over my chest, waiting. I don't push him. I don't try to fight. I just wait, wanting him to know that I'm not leaving, but I'm not going to push until he's ready.

"Care for a drink?" he asks, setting his glass down and pouring himself another.

"No, thanks. After last weekend, I'm kind of over drinking anything hard."

"I have some wine in the fridge," he offers, refusing to look at me.

I shake my head. "I didn't come for a drink, Callan. I came for an explanation. I don't deserve this. If you have a solid reason for why I should be fired, then fine, tell me, and I'll be on my way. But I refuse to be treated poorly when I've done nothing wrong."

He lifts his glass, swallows it all in one gulp, and turns to me. "I'm sorry, Val. You've done nothing wrong."

My mouth drops open as my eyes grow wide with surprise. Not surprise at his answer, but surprise that he's admitting he has no legitimate reason to fire me.

"Then why?" I ask, moving closer to him, slowly.

8

CALLAN

Watching her slowly walk toward me, there's only one thing I want to do. I want to pick her up against me and press her back to the wall while I take everything I need.

Don't do it, Callan, I tell myself. *No good can come from this. You'll fuck her a couple of times until the craving passes, then you'll end up leaving and breaking her heart. You'll have to deal with Bennet and maybe losing your job.*

"Val, I..." I breathe out, shaking my head and rubbing my temples. My thoughts are swirling.

"What is it?" she asks, closing the distance between us.

Do it. Take her. God, I want to be inside her so fucking bad, I can taste it. She's right there, within reach. Just reach out and take her.

"Valerie, I just..." I'm torn: do what my body wants or listen to my brain? The thoughts and emotions are mixing together, only confusing me more.

"What, Callan? Just tell me," she says, her voice soft and sweet. It teases me. It speaks to the monster deep inside of me.

My eyes close. I'm losing the battle with myself.

She reaches out and touches my hand, and my eyes pop open,

landing on hers. They're brilliant green, filled with confusion and innocence.

"Fuck," I whisper, feeling my resolve crumble. I reach for her, my hands finding her hips and pulling her flush against me. In the same instant, I step toward her, my lips landing on hers as we stumble backward. With my left hand on her lower back, I stretch the other one out behind her, catching us as he hit the wall. I kiss her hard and deep, letting myself get carried away by her sweet taste, her heavenly scent, her soft skin that feels like silk.

At first, she's frozen and doesn't respond, but when my tongue demands entrance, she loosens up. Her body molds to mine as her arms wrap around my neck. Her responding to my touch makes my body feel like it's been set on fire, and I pick her up against me, where she wraps her legs around my hips.

Our kiss is hard and fast, but not rushed, just needed. My hands want to touch every inch of her body, but all they seem to do is make their way from her hips to her face, where I cup her cheeks and hold her against me in fear of her pulling away. I don't want her to pull away. I want her to need this as badly as I do.

Her hands begin to slide down my chest, and I think she's about to push me away, but to my surprise, her fingers grab the bottom of my shirt and she pulls it upward. I quickly jump to help her tug it off the rest of the way. Our kiss breaks away for only a moment, but she pulls me right back in. This time, her hands are cupping my face while she takes the kiss deeper.

Inside, I want to cheer because she's not stopping me from taking what I want, but I'm so lost in the moment that I can't think of anything but how badly I need to slide inside her. I force away all thoughts and decide to live in the moment; we'll deal with the repercussions later.

My hands begin pushing her shirt up her stomach, but she quickly reaches for it, tearing it off and tossing it into the floor. We're both breathing heavy, our chests moving up and down quickly. I pull back slightly and look into her green eyes. They're glassy and sparkling, her lips red, swollen, and parted. She looks drop-dead sexy, and just seeing her this way has me nearly busting the seam in my jeans.

I close the space between our mouths once again, placing my hands under her ass to support her weight as I walk us from my office up to my room, where we fall onto the bed. I work my way down her body, pressing kisses to her jaw, neck, and down her chest while my hands get busy stripping her of her bra. I toss the fabric to the floor and pull back to look over her amazing tits. They're big and full, but they fall naturally, unlike the girls I've been with that have fake tits. Hers jiggle and bounce and look so soft. I lick my lips with a slight grin as I lower my mouth to her hard nipple, sucking it into my needy mouth. She lets out a deep moan the moment my tongue flicks against it. Her fingers thread into my hair, pulling at the root but pushing my head against her like she never wants me to stop.

My hands massage her tits while my mouth moves back and forth between them. The whole time, she's breathing heavy and whimpering, making sounds that shoot straight to my painfully hard dick. She must feel it twitch against her because her hands move to my waist, where she starts unbuttoning my jeans and working them down my hips.

I catch her hands in mine and pin them up above her head, looking into her eyes. "I'm in charge tonight. I've been thinking about this far more than I should, and I have to get you out of my system," I tell her, releasing her wrists to strip her of the rest of her clothing. Even though I'm no longer holding her hands down, she leaves them right where I want them.

"Don't move," I demand as I pull her jeans down her legs, leaving her pink, lacy panties in place. I toss her jeans into the floor and position myself between her long, tan, shapely legs. I bend down, pressing a soft kiss to her stomach, next to her belly button. My hands slide under her ass, squeezing and massaging as I kiss my way lower. I gently nip the skin covering her hip bone, and she lets out a whimper.

I kiss my way down her inner thigh, along the line of her panties. I inhale deeply, enjoying her sweet scent.

"Callan, please do something. I'm about to explode," she says around heavy breaths.

Too impatient to remove myself from her to pull down her panties, I move them to the side and run my tongue between her folds. She lets out a deep breath, and her body seems to crumble, her knees closing around my head.

I can hear the way she's breathing loud and heavy but having my head between her legs is more pleasurable to me than she can imagine. I suck her hard nub into my mouth and flick my tongue against it over and over until she's calling out my name. When I slide my finger inside her, her hands fist the pillows, causing me to realize that she still hasn't moved her arms. That pleases me to no end. I like a woman that can take orders in the bedroom.

When her release ends, her muscles ease and her whimpers quiet, but her breathing is still out of control. I pull myself away and lean over to grab a condom out of the bedside table. She keeps her eyes locked on mine as I unzip my jeans and work them down my hips. When I look down to slide the condom on, she does the same, fully taking me in. Her eyes widen, and she licks her lips.

"Like something you see?" I ask, finally pulling her panties down her thighs.

She bites her bottom lip and nods.

I lower my body back onto hers, and I cup her cheek as I kiss her soft and slow. I'm so wound up that I could explode at any minute. I need to slow down, regain control over myself. I feel her knees shaking on either side of me, and it reminds me of how much she needs me. Using one hand, I position myself at her entrance. With a roll of my hips, I'm sliding deep inside her, causing us both to let out a relieved breath. She's so hot and so tight around me, I know I can come at any second. It takes me a moment to regain my composure. When I'm completely inside her and can go no further, I rock my hips against hers, making her call out. Slowly, I withdraw myself, only to thrust back inside.

My heart is pounding, and my breathing is rushed. I have no choice but to break our kiss so I can maintain consciousness.

"Fuck, Valerie," I whisper, moving in and out of her.

Her hands are on my biceps, squeezing as I continue to thrust inside her.

"Callan," she whispers my name, and the sound leaving her lips is life-changing.

I quickly pull out of her and flip her over. She gets onto her knees and bends down before me. All I can see is her firm ass as I use my hand to spread her wetness down between her folds. Slowly, I rise and enter her from behind. With the position change, she feels even tighter around me. I rear back and thrust inside so deep my hipbones dig into her ass. My balls slap off her of skin, and we both call out. Based on the way she's moaning into her pillow, I know that move felt way too good to the both of us, so I repeat the process again and again, causing the wooden headboard to smash against the wall.

I can hear my own heartbeat, our loud moans, the slapping of our skin, and the headboard bouncing off the wall every time I push inside her. I'm gone, completely lost and unable to think about how wrong this is. It feels too good to be wrong. It feels right, like she was made specifically for me. The way our bodies connect, it's like puzzle pieces. I've connected with many pieces over the years, but none of them fit quite as perfect as this one does.

I feel her muscles squeeze my dick, like she's milking it for every drop. Finally, I can't hold back any longer, and I let my release go. It's so strong that my whole body goes completely numb. My muscles seize and lock up, and I can't breathe or do anything until every drop has left my body. My hips begin twitching against her, finishing as I float back down into my body.

I pull out of her, and she collapses onto her stomach. I throw myself down on the bed beside her, remove the condom, and toss it into the nearby trash can. We both stay completely still, letting our hearts calm and our breathing even out. Before I can even move, the guilt of what I've just done cripples me.

I close my eyes, trying to push the thoughts away, but all I can see is the look I know Bennet will give me when he finds out. I try to think of an excuse: I was drunk, she seduced me. Neither sounds good enough to excuse what I've done. I don't think there is an excuse good enough for fucking your best friend's little sister.

Before I can think too deeply on the matter, I drift off to sleep.

———

I STIR wake sometime later and find myself wrapped around her. My right arm is under her head, and my left arm draped over her side. She has one leg between mine and the other over my hip. She's facing me, putting us nose to nose. The only thing covering us is a thin white sheet that only comes up to our waists. Her chest is bare and exposed. And even though I feel guilty for taking something that wasn't mine to take, I can't think of anything but wanting to do it again.

Her eyes open and lock on mine, but neither of us says a word. We can only look at the other and try to figure out how we got here and how to keep it going without anyone knowing. Without saying a word, she moves to sit up, and I roll over to my back, giving her the room she needs to get up and get dressed. But to my surprise, she doesn't leave the bed, she moves onto my body, straddling me.

Instantly, I'm hard and ready to go again. She lifts her hips and uses her hand to slide me inside her. I let out a deep moan from being in her with nothing between us, and she allows her head to fall back, eyes looking at the ceiling. Slowly, she lifts herself, then lowers herself back down my length. But before she repeats the process, she rolls her hips, causing my dick to rub against that perfect spot inside of her. My hands move to her hips, egging her on and enjoying every second of watching her move on top of me. I can't do anything but hold onto her and watch as her tits bounce and her hips roll.

When she slides up my dick, I thrust up into her while pulling her down against me, making her let out a loud moan. God, just the fucking sounds she makes has me want to come undone. But being able to watch as she enjoys my body as much as I enjoy hers, it's enough to have me losing all control.

I hold myself back until she's ridden out every last wave of her release, and when mine bubbles to the surface, I try pushing her away.

But instead of sitting back and letting me release it, she sits on my thighs and uses her hand to jack me off until I'm spilling everything that's left.

Without a word, she stands and walks to the bathroom. I hear the water running, but she quickly shuts it off and comes back with a small towel. She wipes me clean, then tosses it into the floor, laying at my side once again. I want to ask her what's going on with us. I want to ask her if she's as confused as I am, but I'm afraid that talking will break the spell, leaving us with an awkward situation to figure out.

Instead of asking any of the questions troubling my mind, I wrap myself around her, pulling her against my chest, and we both drift back to sleep.

9

VALERIE

I'm not sure what just happened. I'm not sure how we got here. I'm not sure how I feel about it. How could we have crossed such a hard line so fast? There was a time when I couldn't even think about sleeping with Callan. Just the thought alone would cause me to feel sick at my stomach. But here I am, completely naked and wrapped in his arms. And to be honest, it feels pretty good.

Was this just something he did to distract me from getting the answers I was demanding? Or is this the answer to my question? Has he been pulling away because he's had these feelings for me, or is it just another random hook-up for him? I know Callan. He doesn't do relationships. But, I guess that's okay with me because I don't either. God, I'm so confused.

Neither of us are talking. I wonder if he's just as confused as I am about this whole thing. Eventually, I drift off to sleep.

———

I WAKE SOMETIME in the night and Callan is still holding me close. Only now, my back is to his chest. His arm is still under my head, and the other is wrapped around my waist. His hand is only inches away from my clit. Just knowing that we're together, and naked, his hand almost touching me, has me fired up again. I try scooting closer to him as I wiggle my ass against his groin. To my surprise, his cock twitches against me. His left hand flattens out against my stomach, and I feel a sigh leave my lips, thinking what a shame it is that his hand moved further away. But then slowly, it starts moving downward.

It glides down my stomach, across my hip, and to my thigh. Softly, he picks it up and pulls it backward, so it's dangling over his legs, leaving me wide open. Then his hand moves between my hip bones and down to my clit. My whole body twitches when his fingers slide between my folds. His hand works me over before he slides into me from behind. His hips buck up into me while his hand keeps moving against my clit. The arm that was beneath my head moves down to my neck so he can massage my breast while he fills me. Just as my release explodes over me, his does too, but this time, he doesn't pull out. He keeps thrusting into me, and I feel the exact moment when his seed rushes out of him. His hips slow, his breathing slows, and he relaxes behind me again, wrapping me in his arms and holding me close.

In the morning, I wake when I feel him move from behind me. I roll over and stretch.

"Good morning," I whisper, causing his eyes to pop open and lock on mine.

"Morning," he says. "Did we..." he starts but shakes his head.

"Did we what?" I ask, wondering if he has somehow forgotten all the things we've done since we've been together.

"Did we have sex again during the night? I remember something." His brow furrows.

I nod. "I woke up with your hand between my legs." I can't hold back the smile that remembering it brings on.

He nods. "That's right. I remember now. I thought it was a dream," he laughs out. "I was fucking beat." He rubs his eyes with the palm of his hand, then freezes. "I was still partially asleep. I didn't use a condom or pull out." Panic is written all over his face.

"Yeah, I was pretty out of it too, but don't worry. I've got the implant," I say, getting up and walking to the bathroom, noticing the soreness between my legs.

I close the door between us and lean against it. The memories of last night rush back in. I slept with Callan. I fucking slept with Callan. What the fuck am I going to do? Fucking Maddie was right.

Oh, God. What if Bennet finds out? My heart begins to race. It occurs to me that I need to get out of here. The last thing I said to Maddie was I was coming over here. I'm sure she told Bennet, and nobody has heard from me since.

I quickly use the bathroom and wash my hands. I walk back into the bedroom to find Callan just climbing out of bed, completely naked and hard as fuck. Seeing his glorious body causes me to freeze and openly take him in. He offers up a grin as he walks toward me, swagger rolling off of him.

"I like what I see too," he says, pulling me against him for a kiss while his hand gently pinches my nipple. His tongue feels so good moving with mine. I don't know how it's possible to get so lost in a single kiss, but he does that to me. I don't know how it's possible to go from hating one another to fucking, but at this moment, I don't care.

He starts walking me backward, and I suddenly forget that I needed to leave. I forget about how sore I am from our lovemaking last night. I forget everything except the way he makes me feel.

I wrap my arms around his neck and deepen the kiss. The next thing I know, we're in the shower, and he's back where he belongs: between my legs.

Every time I think I'm going to be able to pull away and leave, he reels me right back in. Even though we started in the shower, we finished in the bed, and I roll my way to the edge and stand.

"I really have to go, Callan. I'm starving, and I don't want my mom to worry." I start pulling on my clothes.

He reaches for me. "Wait. No." He grabs my wrist and pulls me back to the bed. "I'll get us something to eat, and you call your mom and tell her you're staying with that friend of yours."

"What is going on with us?" I ask, looking up at him while he's looking over me.

"I told you. You got under my skin. I don't know how or why, but you did. And I haven't been able to get you out of my head since."

"Is that why you moved my desk into the hall?"

He nods.

"And that's why you fired me?"

"I didn't want this to happen. Not because I didn't want you, but because I didn't *want* to want you. You're my best friend's little sister. Bennet would be fucking livid if he found out. I didn't want to break his trust or lose my job. I thought the only way I'd be able to keep my fucking hands to myself would be not to have to see you or talk to you. I tried doing all the right things, but then you showed up here last night." He lets out a deep breath and throws himself back, placing his arm over his eyes. "You just looked so fucking sexy in that low-cut top and those tight jeans. Then you started walking closer, and you smelled so fucking good. Reaching out and touching me was your biggest mistake. I was losing the battle every second, and you walked right into the lion's den."

"So, what does this mean for us?" I ask, voice shaking and unsure.

He shrugs as his arm falls from his face. "I don't know," he breathes out. "I thought maybe if I could get you out of my system, I'd be fine. But here you are, ready to leave, and I still don't want to let you go. All I can think about is how fucking good you feel wrapped around me. Just thinking about it is making me hard all over again." He grabs his dick and works it up and down once.

My eyes are greedy, and I can't help but watch the way he holds himself. I'm fascinated by his length and girth. I've never been with a man so big. No wonder I'm sore. But even though there's pain, it turns me on just remembering why it hurts so much.

"I'll take another one of those sandwiches if you don't mind."

He shoots me a smile. "I'll be right back." He sits up, catches my lips with his, then pulls away to go make lunch.

When I'm alone, I take a deep breath and think about everything he said. Hearing him talk about how turned on he is by me makes me hot all over again. I've never been talked to that way before. The guys I've been with were never really verbal before, during, or after sex.

But with Callan, half of the passion between us is the things he says to me.

I quickly look around for my purse before I remember I left it in my car last night, thinking I wouldn't be away from it long. I quickly pull on his boxers he left in the floor and my tank top before rushing down the stairs and to my car. I pull out my purse and search through it on my way back to the door. I find it to see that I have four missed calls: one from Mom, one from Krista, one from Maddie, and one from Bennet.

I quickly call Krista as I head back to the bedroom.

"Hey, where have you been?" she asks.

"I'm...ugh. I met a guy, and I'm shacking up with him," I finally confess, knowing she'd approve.

"Go you!" she cheers.

"Have you talked to my mom or brother?" I ask.

"No, why?"

"Just checking. I'm going to call them and tell them that I'm with you this weekend. Okay?"

She laughs. "Sure. Have fun and be safe." She hangs up without another word.

I dial my mom's number.

"Valerie, where have you been?" she answers.

I laugh. "Sorry, my phone died. I'm staying with Krista this weekend. Everything okay?"

"I'm fine. I just wanted to check in and make sure you were okay." Concern is drenching her words.

"I'm fine, Mom. I'll see you tomorrow."

Callan walks back into the room, butt naked and holding a tray of food.

"Bye, Mom," I say, hanging up and not waiting for her to respond.

"I made us both our own sandwich this time. I figured we could use the fuel," he says around a laugh.

"I know I could." I pick up my sandwich and take a big bite.

He picks up a chip and pops it into his mouth. "About your brother..." he starts.

"What about him?" I ask around a mouth full.

He slowly looks over at me, his blue eyes finding mine. "You think we can keep this just between us? I mean, there's no reason to tell him, right?"

I nod once. "Right. It's not like we're exclusive or anything."

I see his chest fall when a deep breath leaves his lips. "Okay, good." He leans in and kisses my lips, nipping the bottom one softly as he pulls away. "I'm not quite through with you yet. I hope that's okay?"

"I'm all yours until tomorrow," I promise.

A wicked gleam flashes in his eyes as a smile takes over, and that look makes my stomach tighten with anticipation. Even though he's barely left me this whole time we've been together, I feel empty without him.

We both enjoy our lunch and set the tray off to the side while we cuddle back up. His skin feels good against mine—he's the perfect temperature to keep me warm while also not making me too hot—well, until he wants to, anyway. His hands are strong and firm as they tour my body, teasing every inch they touch. His lips are soft as they kiss along my jaw, breasts, and stomach. And his teeth always nip my skin at the perfect time to have me falling to pieces. No man has ever had this much control over me. Just being beneath Callan makes me want to obey his every command.

My wrists are handcuffed to the bed above me, and my ankles are tied down as well. He's between my legs, but he refuses to give in to my desires. I don't know if he's teasing me or himself more, but either way, we both seem to enjoy it. While his hand gives to me, his other hand works his length up and down slowly. He's rock hard and standing at attention. I can't close my eyes to enjoy the way he touches me though. I have to keep them open to watch the way he touches himself. He removes his fingers from me and presses them against my ass.

"Has anyone been here before?" he asks, corners of his mouth turned up slightly.

I gasp at his touch but shake my head no.

"Can I have it? Can I be the first?"

My nerves skyrocket from his question, but I can't deny him—I don't want to deny him. Everything he's done up to this point has felt amazing. I know all I have to do is trust him.

I bite my lower lip and nod my head up and down.

He slides his finger back into me, wetting it before moving it back to my ass and pushing forward. As his finger slides in slowly, to give me time to adjust, I let out a sound I never heard myself make before.

His half-smile falls from his face as his eyes bounce back and forth between his hand, my face, and back. The hand he has on his dick tightens until his knuckles turn white and he starts moving it up and down even faster.

"Callan, I want you inside me," I cry out, feeling overwhelmed by the pressure and need I'm feeling.

"I already am, baby," he whispers, not stopping what he's doing.

I shake my head no. "Don't stop what you're doing, but fuck me," I plead.

The hand on his dick slows and falls away as he gets himself up to his knees.

10

CALLAN

S he's too goddamn much for me to resist. I keep pushing her, and she keeps taking it. She's just as fucked up as I am. Each time, I take things one step further, thinking this will be her breaking point, but she takes it all and asks for more. She's going to be the death of me. I'm either going to fuck her until I die from exhaustion, or Bennet is going to find out and kill me. Either way, it's all going to be because of her.

I've never in my life spent the entire weekend locked away in my room having sex with the same girl over and over, but that's exactly what we do. We fuck, stop long enough to rest, and start again. Only ever leaving the room to get food, drinks, or to use the bathroom. We sleep, wake up, and do it all again. I know she has to be sore by now because every muscle in my body is throbbing, but even then, I can't fucking stop.

She was nowhere on my radar two weeks ago, and now I can't bring myself to pull out of her. She controls my mind and body. If she's near, I can't stop touching her, kissing her. Even when we sleep, we're touching. This weekend is going down in the books as the weekend I lost myself. The weekend when my life changed.

Sunday morning rolls around, and we're both so sore we can

barely move. We have a quick breakfast in bed, then cuddle up to go back to sleep. When we wake, we finally have to pull apart. We both get dressed, and even though we're happy about the way we spent the weekend, we're both a little sad to be leaving the world we created: a world where it's just us and nobody else.

I walk her down the stairs and to the front door. I open it, but before she can step through, I tug her back for a long, slow kiss. My dick couldn't get hard even if I paid it at this point, but it twitches slightly against her thigh. She pulls away and laughs.

"You're going to kill me."

I smile. "You are killing me."

She walks away, and I hold her hand until our arms can't stretch any further. Finally, I have to let her go. I stand at the door and watch as she climbs into her car and drives out of sight. Finally, I step back in and close the door, looking around my empty house, unsure of what to do.

My back and neck are stiff from lying in bed all weekend. And every other muscle hurts from overusing them again and again. I decide to sink into a hot bath in hopes of easing the pain away. I fill the tub full of hot water and a little Epsom salt, then sink deep beneath the water as I turn on the jets. I lean my head back and close my eyes, breathing deep.

I don't think I've ever in my life been sore from having sex, but I also never had sex ten times in a weekend. I feel like a fucking rabbit. That thought makes me laugh.

My phone rings, and for the first time all weekend, I reach for it.

"Hello?"

"Hey, Cal," a woman says.

"Who is this?" I ask, unsure.

"It's Jennifer. We hung out last Wednesday," she reminds me.

Oh, yeah. Wednesday. "What's going on?"

"I was just calling to see if you wanted to meet up."

I roll my eyes. After this weekend, I can't even imagine hooking up with another woman. "I wish I could, but I can't today. Sorry."

Without another word, I hang up and drop the phone onto the white tile.

———

I GET to the office on Monday and have the maintenance guy move Val's desk back into the office. Then it occurs to me that we didn't talk about work over the weekend. I wonder if she's even planning on coming in. Just as I'm picking up my phone to call her, the doors open, and she walks in.

Her eyes find mine, and she smiles. "Good. I was wondering if you just got rid of the desk completely." She drops her purse onto her desk and turns toward me.

I stand and walk to the center of the room. "I was worried you wouldn't even show up. I was just about to call you."

She shrugs one shoulder. "I figured that after the weekend we had, you would change your mind about firing me."

I laugh and lean in for a kiss that she accepts. With my mouth on hers, I breathe her in deeply, instantly relaxed by her familiar scent. I haven't seen her in twelve hours, but after our time together, it feels more like a week. I didn't even realize that I could miss someone so much.

There's a quick rap on the door, and we shoot apart just before Bennet walks in. His eyes go wide when he sees Val standing next to me.

"Oh, good. You guys made up," he says, motioning toward her desk that's now back in the office.

I nod, and she smiles. "Yeah, I made him un-fire me," she says with a laugh.

Bennet laughs and shakes his head. "Good for you. Maybe we've all learned something from this, and we'll be able to act like professionals around here again?"

"Absolutely," Val says.

"Good. See you guys later," Bennet says, walking out of the office and leaving us alone.

I look down at Valerie and pull her back to my chest. "There's no way, after our weekend, I can be professional."

She places her hands flat on my chest and pushes me away. "Callan, I had a lot of fun with you, but the weekend is over. It's time to get back to work," she insists. Her words are like a slap to my face, but I don't want to let her how much they just gutted me.

I straighten my jacket. "Of course," I agree, walking back to my desk while she goes back to hers. Without another word, we both get to work.

———

WHEN THE WORKDAY ENDS, I go home and change into some casual clothes. As I'm about to walk out of the door, my phone rings. I pull it from my pocket and see that it's my lawyer calling.

"Hey, Troy. Tell me you got something."

"I do. I found Mr. Decon James in Chicago, Illinois. His priors consist of everything from assault to robbery. He was in a juvenile detention center from the ages of sixteen to eighteen, when he was released. He's also done a few overnight stints in jail for some minor things. And the thing I think you're looking for, it turns out that he was accused of rape, but the case was dropped."

"And how does something like that just go away?" I ask, feeling my hand tighten into a fist.

"Well, there could have been no proof, like no DNA was found on the victim, or maybe he had a solid alibi. But in most cases like this, it's because the victim has been paid off."

I nod as anger surges through my body. "Alright, Troy. Thanks a lot. Hey, if you will, email me his info."

"No problem. But, Callan, don't get yourself in trouble."

"Sure thing," I agree, hanging up the phone. I walk out the door and climb behind the wheel. My phone chimes and I open the email Troy just sent. I read over the info and put his address into my GPS.

I'm going to make this guy pay for what he did to her. I'm going to make damn sure to teach him a lesson, make sure he never thinks he can drug a girl to get what he wants ever again.

———

I'M PULLING up to his apartment building a little while later. I shut off the car and climb out, hitting the lock button behind me because I don't trust anyone in this part of town. I let myself into his building and walk up the four flights of stairs until I find his apartment. I knock on the door, and seconds later, it's being swung open.

"Decon James?" I ask, just for confirmation. I remember his face. It's one I'll never forget.

"Yeah?" his brows furrow together.

"Remember me?"

He looks me up and down. "Nah, should I?"

I nod. "I bet you won't forget now," I say, pulling my fist back and landing a hit to his jaw. He falls backward, and I walk into his apartment. I jump down on top of him and hit him a couple more times. Even though he pulls his arms up to cover his face, he passes out, and I take the opportunity to drag him over to the couch and toss him on it. While he's out, I start searching through his things. I look through a bookshelf, surprised the worthless asshole even knows how to read. I open the drawer on the end table and find a wooden box. I pull it out an open it, not surprised to see drugs. There's a bag of weed, a pipe, a bunch of pills, and a vial full of some kind of clear liquid.

I grab the pills and the vial just as he's coming to.

He groans and sits up. "What the fuck," he mumbles, unaware that I'm still here.

I move into his line of sight. "Is this what you used to drug Valerie?" I ask, holding up the vial.

"What? Who?" He's playing dumb.

I pull back my fist and land a hit to his stomach, causing him to fall over onto the couch. "Don't make me repeat myself."

"Alright. Yeah, yeah that's what I used."

I slide it into my pocket. "How many other girls have you used this on?"

"None. I never used it before," he swears. "I wasn't even going to use it on her, but I was fucking tired of her games, man."

"What the fuck are you talking about?" Anger washes its way up to my throat. It burns like acid.

"I've been fucking around with her for months. She'd flirt and make out with me, tease me, lead me to believe that we'd be hooking up, then she'd pull out last minute. I wasn't thinking, man."

"And what about the rape charge you had against you that got dropped?" I ask, still looming over him.

"How'd you...?" he asks, looking up at me with confusion written across his face.

"Answer the question," I demand, pulling my fist back but not swinging it just yet.

"It was a girl I'd been dating. She caught me cheating and was trying to get back at me."

I look down at him, trying to decide if he's telling the truth or not.

"Look around, man. Do I look like I have the money to pay her off?" His brown eyes are wide with fear and seriousness.

I point my finger at him. "If I ever hear of you drugging girls again, you won't have to worry about me kicking your ass cuz' you'll be dead. You better hope the cops find you before I do." Without another word, I leave the apartment, drugs in my pocket.

I don't know why I even bother taking the drugs. He'll just buy more. But taking it makes me feel like I might, at least, save a couple girls while he's trying to get more.

I walk out to the street and walk around the building to the alley. I empty the contents onto the ground, then drop the bottle and crush it with my foot. I still have the pills in my pocket, but I refuse to throw them away where a child could find them. When I get home, I'll flush them. Finally, I turn around and leave.

Instead of going back home, I stop at a Johnie's to grab something for dinner. I'm waiting in a long line outside that stretches the length of the small building to get my Italian beef sandwich and Italian ice, and when I finally get into the small building, I can see out the front windows. My eyes land on Val sitting at the concrete picnic table with another guy. Anger rises in my chest, and it feels like my body has been lit on fire. I turn my back to the window and place my order. A few minutes later, I'm handed a bag and my Italian ice. I walk out the door and around to the front of the building, acting like I didn't see Val sitting there.

"Oh, hey," I say, coming to an abrupt stop.

She looks up at me, her eyes wide and full of fear. But she puts on a fake smile. "Hey, what are you doing here?"

I hold up my bag and take a sip of the lemon-flavored ice. "Just swung by for some food." I look back and forth between her and the guys she's sitting across from. "You on a date?"

Her eyes move from me, to him, and back. "I…we're just hanging out. Brandon is an old friend."

I look over at him in time to see his brows furrow together. His mouth opens, but I see her discretely shake her head no.

I nod. "See ya at the office tomorrow," I say, forcing myself to let it go.

She smiles and waves, but I can tell she's feeling awkward.

11

VALERIE

I wasn't planning on running into Callan while on a date with Brandon, but it's probably good that he saw it. It says what we did was totally casual, right? I'm not the clingy type. I'm not looking to settle down. I'm twenty-one, for fuck's sake. All I want to do is enjoy my youth, have fun. Callan and I had a lot of fun last weekend, and I wouldn't object to doing it again. But based on how he looked at me, he's pissed that I'm with another guy. That confuses me. I thought Callan, of all people, would understand. He's never been the one-woman type.

Brandon walks me to the front door and gives me a quick, polite kiss. "I had a good time tonight."

I nod and smile. "Me too. Thank you."

"I'll call you later?"

I nod. "Sounds good."

When he walks away, I open the door and go inside. Mom is already asleep for the night, so I quietly head downstairs to my part of the house. I drop my purse on the table, then kick off my shoes to get comfy on the couch. After about an hour, I stand to put on some pajamas. I quickly change into a pair of stretchy shorty-shorts and tug on a tank top. When I get back to the couch, there's a text on my phone from Callan.

I'm outside.

I frown at the screen but walk upstairs and open the door to head out, but he's on the front steps. I open the door wider and allow him inside.

"I—" he starts, but I shush him and motion for him to follow me downstairs.

Once we're where Mom can't hear, I turn to face him. "What are you doing here?" I ask, looking up at him. His blue eyes are glassy and bloodshot. It's easy to see he's been drinking.

"I needed to see you," he says, reaching for me and pulling me to his chest. His lips land on mine, and suddenly, everything in my head vanishes. I can't do anything but wrap my arms around his neck and deepen our kiss.

His hands land on my ass, and he picks me up against him. My legs wrap around his hips. He takes a few steps, pressing my back to the wall before breaking the kiss.

"I couldn't sleep," he whispers against my lips. "I thought I could drink you away, but I can't. I had to taste you." He kisses me again, and his words make me melt. I never felt like I meant much to any guy I was with. But Callan, even though we're not technically together, he makes me feel special, like I'm the only one he wants. I don't know if he does this with all his girls, but I don't care. When we're together, it's just us.

"Take me to bed, Callan," I say in a hushed whisper.

His mouth smashes against mine hard before he carries me through the room. "Which one is yours?"

I point in the direction of my room, and he carries me through the door, gently closing it behind us. In the darkness of my room, I can't see anything. But I don't need to because he never stops touching me, kissing me, talking to me.

"I don't know what you did to me, Val. But I can't stop thinking about you," he says, pulling down my shorts as he climbs between my legs. "Every time I close my eyes, all I see is you."

I push his pants down over his hips and his erection springs free. "I need you, Callan," I whisper into the darkness as he positions himself at my entrance.

With one roll of his hips, he slides inside, and we both let out a moan, finally getting what we've been missing.

He pumps into me over and over, making us both call out. The whole time, he holds me close as he claims my body as his own.

He rolls off of me when we finish, and we're both left breathless. There's nothing but silence as we let our bodies get back to normal.

Finally, he breaks the silence. "Who was the guy?"

I shrug one shoulder, the one that's against his so he feels it move. "Just a guy," I reply.

"Are you fucking him?" he asks.

I laugh. "No, it was our first date."

"Did you tell him you're fucking me?"

"What? No!" I turn my head to look at him. "Why would I do that?"

He shrugs and sits up, placing his feet on the floor. "I mean, it's common courtesy, isn't it? If you have a casual relationship, you don't fuck anyone else?" He stands up and pulls up his jeans.

"Whoa, what? A casual relationship? I didn't realize that's what we were doing. I thought we were just having fun." I sit upright, surprised by the sudden turn of events.

"Yeah, I guess we are. But this doesn't seem like much fun anymore, so I'm going to get out of here." He shoves his feet into his shoes and tugs his shirt over his head. "See ya around," he mumbles, walking out of my bedroom.

I wrap my sheet around my body and chase after him. Grabbing ahold of his bicep, I spin him around. "What's gotten into you? You fuck a different girl every night of the week," I point out.

"I used to," he throws in my face. "Until you." His jaw flexes. "I wasn't lying when I said I can't get you off my mind. That isn't just shit I say to everyone."

"Oh," I mumble, feeling like the world is caving in around me.

"I thought we were great together, Val. Imagine my surprise when

I stumble into you on a date with another guy. How would you have felt if that was another girl and me?"

I take a deep breath and think it over. "I don't know, Callan. I…"

"Yeah, that's what I thought. But I guess since you only want me to get laid, I'll leave. Since that part is over now." Without another word, he walks up the stairs and lets himself out.

A part of me feels like shit for hurting him, but the other side says *fuck that.* I didn't do anything wrong. There were no rules when we started this. How was I supposed to know? I pull my clothes back on and head upstairs to lock the door. To my surprise, he's already locked it. I smile to myself. Even when he's pissed as hell at me, he still thinks of my safety.

I head back downstairs to get some sleep.

———

WHEN I GO into the office, I find Callan gone. There's a voice message on the machine, so I press play.

"Val, I'm not going to be in today. I've sent you an email of what I need done. Thanks."

I let out a sigh and can't help but wonder if this has anything to do with last night. But I push the thoughts away and get my work done.

I'm walking out of the office at five and my phone rings.

"Hey, I'm at Bandy's Bar. Come hang out," Krista says.

"Alright," I agree, mostly because I don't want to go home and be alone. I know I'll end up thinking about Callan and how I hurt him.

I grab a taxi and get dropped off at the bar. Krista is already inside with two glasses and a pitcher.

"Shitty day?" she asks when I walk in and collapse in the booth.

"You have no idea." I pick up the pitcher and pour me a glass.

Beer has never been my favorite, but after that night, I want to avoid anything that will impact my judgment that quickly. I'll stick to a couple beers or a glass of wine. That's it.

Krista and I sit and talk for several hours and share one more pitcher of beer. Finally, we leave the bar, both of us getting in separate cabs since we're heading opposite directions.

I sit in the backseat and watch the traffic go by. My mind begins to wander, and of course, it wanders to Callan. I'm halfway home when I tell the cab to turn around.

An hour later, we're pulling up to his house. I slip the driver some money, then walk to his door. I knock a couple of times, and he opens it. He looks at me, and I look at him. He motions with his head for me to come inside, and the second he does, I jump on him, pressing my mouth to his.

He doesn't hold back, even though he's mad at me. It's like he physically can't deny me. He kisses me hard and fast, almost like he was afraid he'd never kiss me again. Finally, he picks me up against him and walks me inside. He presses my back to the door while his hands get busy stripping me of my clothing.

"I'm sorry I got so mad last night," he says against the soft skin of my neck. "I just got so jealous when I saw you with him." He pulls back and looks into my eyes. "You're not mine. I know that."

"Shut up," I say, pulling him back to my mouth so I can devour his.

Without another word, he picks me up and walks me up the stairs.

Something happens when Callan and I are together. The world stops spinning. Nobody else exists. It's just the two of us. I don't worry about work or money or life in general. I can't think of anything but how he can manipulate my body like no one else has ever been able to.

―――――

WE SOMEHOW MANAGE to pull away from one another. We're walking through the house, collecting our clothes so I can leave. He bends down and picks up my shirt.

He hands it over. "I want to take you out, Val."

"Out? Out where?" I ask, tugging it over my head.

He shrugs. "Anywhere. I don't want you to think that I only want you for sex." He cracks a smile.

73

I laugh and shake my head. "You want to take me out on a date?"

He nods. "Yeah, sure. If that's what you want to call it. I mean, even the random women I bring home get dinner or drinks out of me."

I pick up my purse. "Well, that's the difference between them and me. They want something from you. I don't." I press my mouth to his and give him a quick kiss before opening the door and walking out. I pull my phone out of my purse to order a ride home.

"Where's your car?" he asks from the doorway.

"I left it at work. I took a cab," I shout back.

"Come on," he says, walking outside and pulling his keys from his pocket. "I'm not letting you get into a car with a stranger. Haven't you seen all the girls that have gone missing from that shit?" He climbs behind the wheel of his car, and I know there's no point in arguing.

I turn around and climb into the passenger seat. "Thank you."

"For what?" he asks, twisting the key and starting the engine.

"For always thinking of my safety, no matter how mad you are at me."

He scoffs. "You're lucky I'm such a nice guy."

I can't hold back my laugh, not because he's not a nice guy, but because he's always rubbed it in my face, even when he was trying to talk me into eating dirt when we were kids.

I slide my phone back into my purse.

"Want to grab some dinner?" he asks, driving away from his house.

"Sure," I reply.

He laughs.

"What?"

"I knew I'd trick you into a date sooner or later."

I shake my head. "You're impossible."

He nods. "That I am," he agrees.

We walk into a nice restaurant, and we're shown to a table in the corner. We both take our seats, and he orders a bottle of wine for the table. I look around and feel a little awkward. I was raised in places like this, but I haven't seen this side of things in a long time. Since I graduated from prep school. Once I hit college, I forgot about the life of luxury. I traded in my Porsche for a train pass. I sold my name-brand clothes and bought stuff from second-hand stores. My family thought I was crazy, but I really wanted to see the world from a normal person's eyes. I wanted to work for what I had, not be handed everything. Giving up that life was harder than giving up the money. I mean, it only took Bennet a year to talk me into coming to work at the company.

I'm lost in thought when a blonde walks up to Callan.

"Look what we have here," she says, running her fingers up and down his forearm.

He quickly looks up at her. I can tell by the look on his face that she's one of his regulars.

"Where in the hell have you been? I haven't heard from you in a couple of weeks."

He smiles nervously. "Oh, uh. Nikki, this is Valerie. Valerie, this is Nikki. She's um, a friend of mine."

I hold out my hand to shake. "Nice to meet you, Nikki."

"Likewise," she says, sitting down in the open chair between Callan and me. "You mind?" she asks me. "I love this place, and they just told me they're booked." She sticks out her bottom lip. "So, you are saving me from fast food."

I sit back and watch as she talks non-stop. She asks him questions, personal questions, and he laughs and tries dodging them. She leans in when he talks, making sure he has a clear shot down her revealing dress. A time or two, I see his eyes fall to take the cheap shot. The longer this girl sits here, the more annoyed I get. I mean, who does this? Who invites themselves to someone else's dinner? If you ask me, she's trying to swipe Callan out from under me. But Callan and I aren't together.

It's a bitch ass move but he's fair game I guess…I'm the one who said I didn't want anything official. So, why does this bother me?

12

CALLAN

I sit and watch as Valerie's face grows redder by the minute. She goes from calm and collected to shooting Nikki dirty looks when she's not looking. I'm waiting for her to say something, but I think she actually bites her tongue. I can tell when she flinches.

Nikki is a woman I've slept with every Tuesday for as long as I can remember. Half the time, I forget her name and refer to her as Tuesday. Since mine and Val's first encounter, I've been avoiding her. Looks like she finally caught up to me. She's a total flirt, and on more than one occasion, she's even talked me into leaving the girl I was with at the time to go home with her instead. I can tell she's trying that again now, but no way is it going to work. Even though I've slept with her more times than I have Val, Val has something on me. It's like she sunk her hooks into me, and I can't break free, no matter how much I try.

Finally, Val sits up. "Sorry to interrupt, but I really should get going." She pushes back her chair and stands but freezes when I do the same.

Nikki looks up at me with a confused look on her face.

"Sorry, Nik," I say, looking only at Valerie. "But I've got to go." I hold out my hand, and Valerie smiles shyly and takes it.

"But...what?" Nikki asks when we walk away, but I don't stop or turn back.

When we get outside, Val looks up at me. "You didn't have to do that, you know?"

I scoff. "I certainly did have to do that." I open her door and she slides inside.

I walk around and take my seat.

"Why?"

"Because I saw how jealous you were getting. Doesn't feel good, does it?"

"I was not jealous," she argues.

"Oh, really?" I ask, glancing at her from the corner of my eye.

"Really. I was just annoyed. It's impolite to just sit down at someone's table. It doesn't matter if you know them or not. I mean, for all she knew, we could've been on a date."

I laugh. "She didn't care if we were on a date. I've been avoiding her, and she finally caught me."

"Caught you?"

I nod. "I was sleeping with her every Tuesday...up until we started messing around."

Her head quickly turns to look over at me. "Are you saying that you haven't been with anyone else since we've been hanging out?"

I nod. "That's exactly what I'm saying."

I turn to look at her, expecting to see her smile. But instead, she looks freaked out. She slumps down in her seat slightly, and her eyes flash over to look out the passenger side window.

Neither of us says another word on the way to the office so she can get her car. I pull into the parking lot, right next to it.

"Callan," she says, looking over at me, concern painting her face. "We can't get serious. My brother, remember?"

I nod. "I'm not worried about your brother, Val." I lean toward her. My hand cups her cheek, and I pull her in for a kiss. "You're worth it," I whisper.

"You want to be exclusive?" Her brows pull together as a confused look takes over.

I smile and let out a deep breath. "I don't know, Val. I'm confused. I've never wanted this with anyone, but I can't get you off my mind. That has to mean something, right?"

She nods. "Yeah, it means were good in bed together. That's it. I've never been in a serious relationship, Callan." Her words are rushed. I can tell she's freaking out from my confession.

"Well, have you been with anyone else since we started...you know?"

She shakes her head.

"I think that's your answer, Val. What we're doing now, it will be no different."

She takes a deep breath and lets it come out in a rush.

Again, I lean over and kiss her. "Just think about it. No pressure."

She nods and exits the car. I sit back and watch as she climbs into her own and drives off.

Any other woman, and they'd be head over heels that I want to commit. But Val, she's something else. She's like the female version of me. And here I am, a guy that sleeps with more women in a week than some guys get in a year, and I'm asking for more. No wonder she's freaked out. She doesn't know if she can trust this, trust me.

I decide that even if she tells me she doesn't want to be exclusive, I'm going to hold out hope. Make her see that she can trust me. Make her want me as badly as I want her.

On my drive home, I think about her some more, wondering why she's so different. She's beautiful, kind, down to earth, and not a spoiled brat. She knows what she wants, and she doesn't settle for less. And somehow, she's managed to overlook our fucked up past. She sees the guy I am, not the boy I was.

Instead of driving home, I make a last-minute turn and swing by a private club. It's not a dance club. It's more of a wealth club. Everyone has to pay twelve grand a year to have a key. A single glass of bourbon runs about twenty-seven bucks. But it's a place we can go to get away and be around people with similar problems.

I use my key to let myself in the door. There's some light jazz music playing in the background as I take a seat at the bar.

"How you doin', Cal?" Jeanie asks as she places a coaster down on the bar for my drink.

"I'm doing good," I say. "Can I get a glass of scotch?"

"Of course." She quickly walks away to pour my drink.

I look around me and only find a few people sitting at the tables, no two people together. Everyone is quiet, lost in thought.

Jeanie brings my drink back, and I pass her a fifty. "Keep the change."

She smiles kindly. "Thank you." She leans against the bar. "Have you been fraternizing with the riff-raff? I haven't seen you in a while."

I nod and take a sip. "I guess I have. I met a woman, and we haven't spent much time out of the bedroom, if you know what I mean."

She laughs and playfully smacks my hand. "Tell me about her."

I feel my eyes glaze over when I start thinking about her. "She's tall and thin, and beautiful. She has dark hair and green eyes. She's smart and kind and creative. I don't know what it is, but I can't get her out of my head."

"Sounds like you're falling in love," she points out.

I laugh. "Me? Love?" I shake my head "No."

Her brow lifts as she studies me.

Fuck. Am I falling in love? It can't happen that quickly, can it? Damnit, no wonder Val is freaking out. She can see it too. I'm fucking falling in love with her while she's playing my usual game. How the hell did this happen? I'm always careful. I don't let women get under my skin. I keep them at arm's length. I always leave them wanting more. But this time, Val's left me wanting more, every time she's walked away.

"Hey, I didn't mean to freak you out," Jeanie says, pushing her red hair behind her ear.

I shake my head, finish my drink, and stand. "I have to go," I mumble, rushing back out the door.

I find myself sitting in my office, another drink in hand. I lean forward in my leather chair, resting my elbows on my knees as I watch the flame in the fireplace dance around. The wood pops and cracks, and it helps all other sounds to fade away. My head is empty; not a single thought crosses my mind. Finally, there's peace.

I hear a knock on the door, and I stand to answer it. Pulling it open, I find Nikki on the other side. She smiles and holds out a bottle of Johnny Walker. I laugh and take it, motioning for her to come in with my head. I lead her back to my office, where she takes a seat while I open the bottle and pour us both a glass. I hand her the drink and sit on the leather couch beside her.

She takes a sip, then swirls the liquid. "You seemed off tonight. I wanted to check in."

I shrug. "I'm fine, a little confused, but fine."

She tilts her head to the side as she examines me. "Confused? About what?"

I let out a deep breath. "I started fantasizing about a woman I knew I couldn't have for several reasons. She's someone that is just like us. She doesn't do the relationship thing. I tried to stop myself, but I couldn't. I gave in and took what I wanted. Again and again. And now, something is off. I want to change. I don't want to be single and blowing my way through women. And that scares me. But what scares me more is how I'm feeling about this woman that doesn't seem to want anything but a good time."

Her hand lands on my back, and she lets out a soft laugh. "Oh, Callan. We've all been there a time or two. It just comes with the territory when you are the way we are. We keep people at arm's length. We try to keep our feelings in check, but we're only human. Sometimes, those feelings creep up on us."

"Are you saying you've been in love before?"

She smiles and rolls her eyes. "A few times."

"How'd it work out?" I ask, looking over at her.

"Once I realized how I was feeling, I turned and ran the other way. Eventually, with time and space, all feelings fade away."

"Do they, though, or do you just push them away every time they start creeping back up?" I lean back, setting my glass on the end table.

"Just avoid this woman and you'll see. Every day that passes, you'll think of her a little less, until one day, you don't think of her at all."

I look up just as she's crawling into my lap, straddling me. Her hands cup my cheeks as she looks into my eyes.

"Let me help you forget all about her," she whispers, moving in and pressing her lips to mine.

My head is a bit of a mess, and I don't think about anything but this moment. I let my eyes flutter closed as she kisses me. Her tongue slides into my mouth, and her hips start grading against mine. I breathe her in. I can feel her soft lips, but I feel nothing else. There is no dying need to be inside her like there is with Valerie. There's no tingles, no excitement. There's nothing. I force myself to wait a bit longer, hoping that maybe I'm just drunk and the usual feelings will kick in, but after several long minutes of her kissing me and touching me, I break away.

"I'm sorry, but I can't," I tell her, sliding her off of me and onto the couch. "You should probably go, Nikki."

She looks at me, surprised. I've never told her no before. But once she gathers her emotions, she stands up and leaves without a word. The sound of the front door slamming fills my ears.

I grab my phone and send a text.

Can you come over?

While I wait for a response, I pour another drink.

I hear the door open, and I stand to check it out. Maybe Nikki forgot her purse or something. When I round the corner, I bump into Valerie. My elbow touches her arm, and just that simple touch causes a storm to brew. My emotions are running rampant, lighting every nerve ending, causing tiny explosions and fires to break out through my body.

I look down at her, mouth open with no words coming out.

She smiles up at me. "I was already on my way."

I reach out, placing my hands on either side of her face as I pull her mouth to mine. She kisses me back with passion and excitement as her hands wrap around my neck. I press her back to the wall and look down at her.

"I can't do it anymore, Val," I admit.

"Can't do what?" she asks, voice strained.

"I can't keep seeing other women." I let out a long breath. "When I'm with them, I feel nothing. All I want is you." I kiss her quickly, but then add on, "I don't care if you want to see other guys. But I'm only going to be with you."

Her lips turn up into a smile. "I don't want to see anyone else, Callan. I don't know if we'll work, but I do know that nobody else can compare to you."

I smash my mouth against hers and kiss her deeply as relief and happiness wash over me. The fear of Bennet finding out doesn't even cross my mind. It can't, because when I'm with her, I only see her.

13

VALERIE

ONE MONTH LATER...

THE WORKDAY IS ALMOST OVER, and I couldn't be more ready. All day long, I've had to sit across from Callan while he sends me sexy text messages of all the dirty things he promises to do to me tonight. Every muscle is tense from trying to hold off the flood of passion that he causes me to feel.

I shut off my computer and grab my purse just as he's walking toward the door. His hand is on the knob, but he doesn't move to open it. He places his other hand on my cheek. "I'll see you at my place?"

I nod as a smile takes over. "I'll be there soon," I promise.

"Not soon enough," he whispers, lowering his mouth to mine.

He kisses me softly, but deeply. Before, when Callan kissed me, it was hard, rough, strong, but here lately, his kisses have been soft, deep, and long, like he can't get enough of me, like he wants to savor every second of it, burn every last detail into his memory.

A knock on the door makes us shoot apart just before he opens it.

Bennet is on the other side. He walks in and turns to face the two of us. "I need a favor, and I didn't know who else to ask," he breathes out.

"What's going on?" I ask.

"You've heard of Geo Halsing, right?" he asks, looking at Callan.

He nods. "Yeah, he's the kid that just inherited his father's billion-dollar estate, right?"

Bennet nods. "Exactly. Well, I had a meeting set up with him because he's wanting to pull every cent." He shakes his head. "We can't lose an account that large, Cal."

"Alright. What do you want us to do?" I ask.

Bennet's eyes jump from me to Callan, and back. "This guy is only twenty-one and doesn't have one business bone in his body. If he takes this money, he's going to live large for a few years, but he will blow every last penny. I need help talking him into leaving it with us. Letting us invest it and use it with the promise of a return. I thought everything was going according to plan, but it turns out he's just too busy to come in and talk about business because he's only here for a vacation. I got word that he's going to be hitting up Hanger 10 tonight."

"Alright, I'll help you rope him in," Callan agrees.

Bennet looks at us both. "Well, actually…and I hate to do this, but Val, do you think you could, you know, use your womanly wiles on him? Make sure he dances, drinks, has a good time. Then me and Callan push him to sign?"

I look up at Callan and even though he's trying to maintain his composure, I can see the annoyance breaking through. His jaw flexes and his nostrils flare.

"I don't know, Bennet. I mean, I don't do the whole club scene anymore. Not after…you know."

Bennet's eyes stretch wide. "I know, Val. But I'll be there, and Maddie, and Callan. Nothing could possibly happen. We need this client. His dad started this business deal up twenty years ago with nothing but a grand. In that time, his investments have done so well, his account now stands at more than twenty millions dollars." He shakes his head. "We can't lose that kind of money in one quarter. The board will be all over my ass."

I take a deep breath, wanting to help, but not wanting to be back in that scene. "Why can't Maddie do it?" I ask.

"Maddie is my wife, Val. There's no way I'm going to let her dance with another guy, having to sit back and watch as he puts his hands on her, even innocently."

I laugh. "But it's okay for your little sister?"

"You're single, and this is your usual thing anyway. Cal and I will be there. All you have to do is tell us when, and we'll stop everything," he promises.

"Fine, but I'm getting paid for this. If I have to work after work, I want double my pay for every hour I'm there. I also want the bonus you're supposed to get with every signature. Got it?"

He nods. "Deal. Thank you. The club opens at ten." He rushes out the door.

Callan shuts it behind him and shakes his head. "I don't like this," he admits.

"Me neither, but like Bennet said, you guys will be there to make sure this guy behaves."

He steps up to me and pulls me to his chest. He doesn't kiss me or touch me provocatively; he just hugs me close. I can hear the way his heart is pounding against his chest.

I look up at him, cupping his cheek. "I'll be fine," I promise, leaning in and pressing a kiss to his mouth.

———

WE GET TO THE CLUB, and the place is packed and very loud. It's so crowded that I find it hard to move and even breathe at times. Memories flood over me: dancing with Decon, getting close in the booth, then the memory from the next day of being sick and in pain. Just remembering it all puts me on edge and makes me feel angry.

Luckily, Bennet sprung for the VIP area, so we at least have our own place to sit to get away from the crowd.

Bennet and Callan sit on the ends of the booth with Maddie and me between them. Under the table, Callan places his hand on my thigh. Just a simple touch eases away the anxiety I feel. I take a deep breath and try to resist leaning into his side.

This past month with Callan has been great. We spend all our free time together, and I don't feel as if I'm missing out on anything by not going on dates with other guys. I never thought I'd be the relationship type, but I guess you just have to find the right one. I try not to over-think it though, because then a sudden panic rises in my chest when I consider what we're really doing, how much trouble we could get into with my brother.

I reach under the table and place my hand over his, letting him know that I'm grateful for his touch, his support and understanding through all of this.

We all order a round of drinks, and while everyone else is throwing them back, I'm only sipping on mine here and there. I still haven't gotten over my issues with drinking and being back in the club only makes me want to avoid it more.

Maddie and I sit and talk about everything from our nails to things going on at work. Bennet is watching everyone that comes through the door like a hawk, and Callan is sitting next to me, body tensed. Hours go by, but I finally finish my drink and can no longer feel my legs from sitting still so long.

"Excuse me," I say, edging my way out.

Callan stands up. "Where are you going?" he asks.

"What do you care?" I ask, noticing that Bennet and Maddie are both watching our exchange.

He seems taken aback for a moment, then notices the two people staring at us. "I don't," he says, sitting back down.

I head back to the bathroom and wait in the line. I rest my shoulder against the wall and pull out my phone, sending him a quick text.

I'm waiting in line for the bathroom.

Want me to wait with you?

I laugh. *No, I think that would be a little weird, wouldn't it?*

After waiting a few minutes, I slide the phone back into my purse.

Finally, I use the bathroom, and when I walk out, I see Bennet standing up. He's talking with a guy that I don't know. I assume it's the guy we've been waiting for, so I head over.

I stop next to Callan and Bennet.

"Here she is," Bennet says, turning him to face me. "She can tell you every place you need to see while you're here. She knows where all the parties are happening."

The guy looks up at me and smiles. "Ah, nice to meet you. I'm Geo." He holds out his hand.

I force a smile onto my face and shake his hand. "I'm Valerie."

"Very beautiful name. Are you free for the night?"

I nod. "Would you like to get a drink?"

"Absolutely," he replies, holding out his arm.

I slip mine through his and lead him toward the bar.

As we sit and wait for his drink, he looks over the club, and I can't help but check him out. He has naturally darker skin—maybe of Italian descent— his sleek dark hair is kept in a gentlemen's cut, and he has dark brown eyes. He's only about my height, and he doesn't have much muscle mass to him. His eyes are wide, taking it all in.

"So, you come here often?" he asks, turning his attention back to me.

I shrug. "I used to, but it's been a while. I've been too busy with work."

"Oh, where do you work?"

I point over at the table. "Windsor Wealth Management." He's handed his drink. "We should get back."

I stand and walk back to the table, and he follows me. Maddie and I sit and talk while Bennet and Callan talk to him about his investments. I listen to them go through the whole thing before getting bored and turning toward Maddie.

"Is there something going on with you and Callan?" she asks low, so nobody else hears.

"What? No! Why would you think that?" I ask, picking up my water and taking a drink.

"I just picked up on some things. Like him asking where you were going when you went to the bathroom. And the moment this guy walked in and his eyes landed on you, Callan started to look angry. Then when you were at the bar, he didn't take his eyes off you. He was watching you like a hawk."

I wave my hand through the air. "I think he's just a little worried based on the last time he saw me in a club. He's not going to let me out of his sight. If it had been Bennet that night, he'd be the same way right now."

She shrugs one shoulder but dismisses her thoughts.

"Valerie!" someone shouts from across the table, and I look up to find Geo looking at me. "Care to dance?"

I look at Bennet, and his eyes widen and his head motions for me to go. I glance at Callan, and he's standing up straight, jaw cocked and eyes fixated on something above my head, like he's just dazing off into space, trying not to pay attention.

I force that smile back onto my face. "Sure," I agree.

I stand up, and he takes my hand, leading me onto the dance floor.

I spin around, and he pulls me close as we move together to the beat of the music. His hands are on my hips, and his eyes are locked on mine. I place my hands around his neck and smile a little bit, reminding myself that I have to make this guy enjoy himself for the company's sake.

We dance through one song, and when it ends, I go to walk back to the booth, but he isn't done, and he pulls me back. I let out a quick shriek when he spins me around and catches me against his chest. He smiles wide, and I laugh.

"You are a very beautiful girl," he tells me, eyes slowly moving up and down my body.

"Thank you. You're very sweet," I reply.

"How has someone not scooped you up already?"

I shrug one shoulder while continuing to dance. "I'm not much for relationships. I prefer to stay single and have fun."

His smile turns into a wicked grin. "My kind of girl." He pulls me closer, and his hands move toward my ass just a little. Not enough to make me think he's grabbing my ass, but enough that I noticed they've moved. "What do you say to coming back to my hotel with me?"

Fuck. What do I say to that? No, obviously, but how can I let him down easy? Make it to where Bennet doesn't lose him as a client?

"I guess we'll just have to see where we end up at the end of the night," I say around a coy smile.

When the song ends, I fan my face and pull away. "I'm going to get a drink."

"I'll join you," he says with a wink, following along behind me.

I take my seat back between Callan and Maddie and the guys attack him again, wanting to talk shop. But this time, he doesn't even pay attention to them. Instead, he watches me with a smile.

14

CALLAN

It's fucking pissing me off the way he's looking at her. And it pisses me off even more that I can't do anything about it. If I even look like I'm getting mad, I'll have to explain myself to Bennet, and I have no clue what I'd even say. I can't believe he asked her to do this. I mean, it's not like he's pimping her out or anything, but it's just the fact that he asked her to come into a club after the thing that happened last time. She's clearly not comfortable here. She won't hardly even drink anymore. She doesn't talk a lot about that night, but I know it still fucks her up. Just sitting here between Maddie and me, she looks worried, stressed, and scared. I hate seeing her like this.

"Listen, Geo. Your dad, he trusted us for many, many years with his investments. He only put in a grand, and we changed that to over a quarter of a million dollars. If you sign this paper and leave this money with us, you'll never have to worry about retirement. You'll be able to live large up until the day you die," Bennet says, still trying to sell this guy on not pulling out of the company.

He nods like he's listening to him, but his eyes never leave Valerie. So I decide to show him what all is around him.

I put my arms around his neck. "Look at all these fine women here tonight, Geo. See that busty blonde over at the bar? I bet it'd only take a drink with her to get her to leave with you. Or that redhead on the dance floor. Look at the way she moves them hips. You know that'll be a good time. You could have a lifetime of this if you play your cards right." He looks at the women I point out, and he smiles and nods. But for some reason, he looks back at Valerie.

"What about you?" he asks her.

"What about me?" she asks, eyes wide as they flash from him to me, and back.

"Would you come back to the hotel with me if I bought you a drink?"

Val laughs but nervously looks down to her water.

"Hey, she's not going home with you tonight," I say, turning him around back to the crowded bar.

But he shakes his head. "They all look nice, dude. But the one I want is already sitting at our table." He smiles and turns back around to look at her some more. He holds out his hand. "Come on, Valerie. Dance with me some more."

I take a deep breath and slowly let it out, hoping to keep my anger in check.

She stands, and they both walk onto the dance floor.

I sit back down, and Bennet picks up his drink, tossing it back. "I think we may have lost him."

I nod. "Who gives a shit? You see the way he's objectifying your sister?"

He scoffs. "He's not doing anything but dancing with her. It's nothing that neither of us haven't done a million times."

"But she's your sister!" I motion toward them.

"Cal, you need to chill. He's flirted and danced: that's it. He hasn't touched her inappropriately; she hasn't had to tell him to stop. She's fine. Val knows how to handle herself."

I sit back and grit my teeth, nostrils flaring. When I turn my head, I find Maddie staring at me with a grin.

"What?" I ask.

She forces her smile away. "Nothing," she replies as she picks up her drink and finishes it off. "Baby, would you get us another round?" she asks, handing over her cup.

He nods and stands to head to the bar.

Maddie scoots closer. "You and Val, you have something going on, don't you?"

I look over at her. "What? No! Why would you think that?"

She laughs. "That is exactly what Val said. But I can tell. You're being awfully protective of her."

I shrug. "It's nothing more than what I'd do for you, Mads."

She rolls her eyes. "Sure it is, and we both know it. I'm not going to tell Bennet. It's none of his business who his sister is seeing."

About that time, I see Valerie come walking back toward the table. She looks pissed and has Geo following along behind her in a rush.

"I'm sorry, Val. I thought we were having a good time," he says, grabbing her arm and spinning her around.

I quickly jump up, pushing him back and pulling Val behind me. "What's going on?" I ask.

"This asshole thought he'd try seducing me into going back to his hotel with him," she says, stepping to my side. "I won't even repeat the nasty things he said to me."

"You what?" I ask, stepping forward.

"She's very beautiful. I was just complimenting her," he says with a grin, not at all afraid of me. It's clear that he doesn't know the proper way to treat a woman.

"He told me I was one fine piece of ass, then he stuck his tongue in my ear," Val says, eyes wide with surprise.

I step toward him as I'm drawing my fist back, but Bennet runs up just in time. He holds me back with both arms. "Hey, what the fuck is going on?"

"This asshole is treating your sister like she's a whore," I yell, still trying to get at him.

"Cal, just chill and let me talk to him," Bennet says.

With a deep breath, I stop trying to push my way through Bennet and give him the chance to fix this.

"What happened, Valerie?" Bennet asks, looking over at her.

Geo steps up. "This is fucking bullshit. You brought a lady to keep me happy, didn't you?"

I jump toward him again, but Bennet catches me.

"No, I brought someone you could hang out with, get some tips on where people your age flock to. I didn't bring my sister for you to sleep with," Bennet spits out.

Geo's face contorts as he shakes his head. "Fuck this. I'm done with all of you. My lawyer will be in contact with you soon about getting my money." Without another word, he walks off.

"Goddamn it, Callan," Bennet yells, turning his angry eyes back to me. "What the fuck is your problem? You just cost us over twenty million dollars." His brows are arched high, arms held out.

"The way he was treating Val may be okay in your eyes, but it's not in mine," I say, shaking my head.

"If she was uncomfortable, she should have come to me. I would've been able to put a stop to it without losing that account! You need to get ahold of yourself. And since when are you her keeper?" He points over at her, standing next to my side.

I look down at her, and she looks up at me.

He looks at the both of us. "No," he says around a laugh, causing us to both look back at him.

He shakes his head. "No way. You two?" he asks, motioning toward the two of us.

Neither of us deny it nor confirm it.

His smile begins to fade, morphing into a tight line as his eyes narrow on me. "You're fucking my little sister?" he asks more quietly, stepping toward me.

"Ben, man..."

He shakes his head again and walks off. Maddie grabs her purse and chases after him, leaving us alone.

We leave the club, and neither of us talk on the ride home. She walks into the house before me, and I follow her up the stairs and into my room. She stops at the dresser, slips out of her shoes, and beings removing her jewelry.

I walk into the closet to strip out of my clothes. I walk back out wearing only my boxers. "I'm sorry," I breathe out, hanging my head.

She walks up to me and wraps her hands around my neck. "It's not your fault. You were only doing what you promised."

I lean my forehead against hers and inhale her scent deeply. "I'm just worried about what he'll do. I refuse to let you go, Val. This past month, it's the happiest I've ever been." I press my mouth to hers.

She kisses me back, and I pick her up against me, moving us to the bed. We collapse on top, and I crawl up between her legs. She breaks our kiss and pushes against my chest until I roll over. Then she gets up onto her knees and starts removing her dress.

"You know, I never thought we'd make it this far," she admits.

I pull my arms behind my head, holding it up so I can watch her.

"I knew that we were magical when we were together, but I never thought that either of us would be this happy. We were both a little wild." She reaches behind her and unzips her dress. It falls to the bed, and she pulls it away, slinging it to the floor. "But now that I know how great we are together, I don't want it to end."

"It won't," I whisper, cupping her cheek and directing her lips to mine. "I swear, Val, it doesn't matter what he does or says: I'm not letting you go. You hear me?" I roll us over, claiming my spot between her legs.

I open my eyes and see her nod, a small smile appearing.

"What if he fires you?" she asks as I kiss my way down her neck.

"If he fires me, I'll get another job." I kiss her collarbone.

"What if he wants to fight?" she whispers.

"Then I'll let him beat the shit out of me, but I won't let you go." I unhook her bra and suck her nipple into my mouth. It hardens with my touch, and she lets out a soft whimper.

I slide my hand down her panties, and my fingers glide between her folds with ease. Feeling how wet and ready she is for me excites me. "Fuck, Val. You're always ready for me," I whisper against her skin as my lips work their way lower.

She lets out a soft giggle. "All you have to do is touch me, Callan."

———

I OPEN my eyes in the morning, and the first thing I see is her. She's sound asleep, dark lashes fanned out across her cheeks. The corners of her mouth are lightly turned up into a smile. I can't help myself. I reach out and gently run the tips of my finger up her bicep. Her eyelids flutter open, and her smile widens.

"Hey," she whispers.

"Hey," I reply, scooting closer, so we're nose to nose.

Her hand comes up, cupping my cheek as she pulls me closer. She presses the softest of kisses to my lips.

"Good morning," I whisper against her lips just before I demand entrance into her mouth.

We kiss long and slow, and just as I'm rolling over to claim my place on top of her, my phone rings. I want to ignore it. I want to keep going. I don't know what it is about her, but she's all I want: all I want to touch, all I want to kiss and hold. The world could end tomorrow, but as long as I have her, I'll be just fine.

"Please, answer that," she says, breaking the kiss.

I groan but roll back over to my side of the bed. "It's Bennet," I mumble, shocked that he's calling.

"What do you think he wants?" she asks, eyes widening as she pushes herself up into a sitting position.

I shrug. "To talk about last night?"

She takes a deep breath, but motions for me to answer.

I push the button and bring the phone to my ear. "Hello?"

"I need you at the office," he says quickly.

"Alright. What's going on?"

"What do you think is going on? We have damage control after your little stunt last night."

A sigh leaves my lips. "Alright. I'll be there soon."

Without another word, he hangs up.

"Well?" she asks with hopeful eyes.

"I gotta go into the office," I admit, moving to stand.

"What? Why?"

"As Bennet put it, damage control from my stunt last night."

She rolls her eyes and scoffs. "What's his deal? Why can't he just let this guy take his money and go? He's a complete asshole."

I sit back on the edge of the bed and place my hand on hers. "If it were just a regular guy, I'm sure he would. But the company will take a serious hit if it loses twenty million dollars in one quarter. As much as I hate this guy and hate to admit it, we need him."

She throws herself back. "Alright. Go, leave me," she says, teasing.

I laugh and crawl back up over her. "I'll be home later. We'll grab some dinner, maybe hit up a movie. Our secret is out. We no longer have to hide behind these walls. We can do whatever we want." I press my mouth to hers.

"Mmm, I like the sound of that," she says around a grin.

"I gotta jump in the shower. Can you start some coffee?" I ask, pulling away and heading for the bathroom.

15

VALERIE

W hen Callan leaves for the office, I take a long hot bubble bath to relax. I grab my phone and call Maddie.

"Hello?" she answers.

"Hey," I breathe out.

"Hey," she replies.

"How'd it go last night, Mads? Is he totally pissed at me?"

She laughs. "He was. But he's come to terms with it."

"Really? Already?"

"Don't get me wrong, he's still pissed about losing that account, and he's not so happy with Callan. He said that if Callan had feelings for you, he should've come and talked to him instead of hiding it. But you, you're his baby sister. You're not in any trouble."

That makes me feel a little better, but I also don't want Callan to be in trouble either. "You think his and Callan's friendship will survive this?"

"I think it will take some time to get them back to how they used to be, but in the long run, I think everything will be okay."

"Okay, Mads. I just wanted to check in and say sorry if I made your night horrible."

She laughs. "Are you kidding me? Bennet was pissed, that's for sure, but he put all that aggression into se—"

"Hey, too much information," I say, cutting her off, which only makes her laugh harder.

"So, to change the topic. You and Callan!"

This time, it's time for me to laugh. "I know. You were right," I admit.

"I knew it the moment we started talking about it. Jazz and my brother were the same way, you know. They hated one another for the longest time. But you know what they say…there's a fine line between love and hate."

"Yeah, but I always thought that meant you could go from loving someone to hating them."

"Shush it; it works both ways." She lets out another giggle. "So, the sex. Spill it. Is he a monster in bed?"

"Madeline Windsor, you're a married woman."

I can practically hear her eyes roll. "So what? Is it hot and passionate?"

I can't hold off my smile. "So good, Maddie. He's sexy and cocky but in a good way. And he never gets enough. I swear, his libido is like a teenage boy."

She laughs. "Sounds like he and your brother have a lot in common."

"Ew! Gross, why would you tell me that?"

"Well, you told me."

"Yeah, but it's not your brother!"

"Alright, I'm sorry. I'll just listen to all your sexy stories and won't tell you any of mine. But, Val, I have some good ones."

I shake my head. "Just tell me it was with another guy and not my brother."

"Deal," she laughs out.

"I'm going to get off of here, Mads. Since Callan is gone for the day, I'm going to get ahold of Krista and see if she wants to hang. I haven't seen her in a while."

"Alright. Have fun but be careful. We all know the messes you get yourself into."

I roll my eyes. "You're starting to sound as bad as my brother."

She groans. "Don't make me the responsible adult."

I laugh. "See ya later."

"Bye." She hangs up, and I drop the phone onto the floor to finish my bath.

When I get out, I dry off and wrap myself in a fluffy robe. As I stand at the counter and fix my hair and makeup, I call Krista.

"Hey, bitch," she answers.

I laugh. "God, I've missed your voice."

"Of course you have. What's up?"

"Callan is busy working today. I figured I'd see if you wanted to meet up. We can grab some lunch and hit the mall or something?"

"Sounds good to me. I have a party to go to later and need to find something hot to wear."

I laugh and shake my head. "I'll be by in an hour?"

"See you then!"

I hang up the phone and finish getting ready. I'm pulling up to her apartment an hour later. I pull to the side of the street and send her a quick text. Moments later, she comes running down, blonde hair flying crazily around her.

"Hi, love," she says, bouncing into the car.

I smile. "Hey, ready?"

"Always." She pulls her seatbelt around herself.

We talk as we head toward the mall. I tell her about dating Callan and how we'd managed to keep it a secret. Then I tell her about my brother finding out and his reaction.

"Really? Bennet?" she asks, scrunching her face.

I nod. "Yep. My brother, the guy that used to go through girls like bubble gum, is now giving me shit for dating a guy just like he was."

"Marriage has changed him."

I laugh. "No, Maddie changed him. I'm not sure any other woman could have done it. I just don't know why he can't look at Callan and me and think I'm just like Maddie to Cal. You know?"

She nods. "You're the one that made him change his ways," she agrees.

"Enough about me. Tell me about you. Who are you seeing? Still messing with Brain?"

She smiles wide and nods. "Yeah, me and Brain are still a thing. But I've met this new guy. His name is Scott. He's super hot and fun to hang out with. Plus, he's rich, and every time we go out, he ends up paying for everything. Which, I know this isn't a big thing to most women, but I've never been with a guy that's already secure in his job. Most of the guys I end up with are crashing on their best friend's couch. It's like I'm a loser magnet."

I giggle. "Are you and this Scott getting serious?"

She shrugs one shoulder. "More serious than I've gotten with anyone else."

"But not too serious since you said you're still messing around with Brain."

"I mean, we have a casual thing going. But the longer it goes on, the more he's calling me."

"What about Decon? Have you seen him lately?"

She nods. "Yeah, every time Brian and I go out, he ends up tagging along. He wonders off as soon as we get to the club though. And he keeps asking about you. Every time, he's all, *where's Val? Is Val coming? Why don't you call her up?*" She rolls her eyes and shakes her head.

"I can't believe he has the audacity to even speak my name!"

"He's something else. And here lately, it's gotten worse. He's asked if I've seen you, your address, where he could casually bump into you."

"You haven't told him, have you?"

"No! Of course not. I'm not stupid."

Just hearing that he's still asking about me pisses me off. I mean, who does that? Who attacks a person, gets away with it, and then continues to ask about them? He's lucky I didn't have any evidence, otherwise, I would have gone to the police. Unfortunately, all I had evidence of was having drugs in my system. It would've been mine and Callan's word against his, and that's not good enough. I don't think the police will play by the playground rules of two against one.

We get to the mall, and we go into nearly every store. Krista finds her perfect outfit for the party, and then we head into the Chinese restaurant on our way out of the mall. I order fried rice and orange chicken, and she orders a sample platter with a big cocktail.

"Are you sure you don't want anything to drink?" she asks.

I shake my head. "I'm scared since that night. Every time I smell alcohol, I get flashbacks from that night, how sick I was, how my head was pounding so bad. My heart starts racing and fear burns its way up my throat. I think I have some serious PTSD."

She offers up a sympathetic look. "It's understandable."

I let out a deep breath. "I wish you'd stop hanging out with those guys, Kris. I mean, you got this new guy. Get serious with him and get out of the club scene. It's dangerous."

She nods and offers up a smile. "I know. I tell myself that all the time."

"Then why don't you?"

"I don't know. I just feel like if I do that, then it's like finally admitting that I'm getting old and growing up."

I laugh. "You're twenty-one, for crying out loud. That's nowhere near old."

She joins in on my laughter. "I know. I just feel like I'm doing what I'm supposed to be doing. You know, acting stupid, enjoying my youth, making mistakes. I'm afraid of settling down and being with one man."

I nod in agreement. "I know, it is scary. Especially after living the way we have been. I mean, up until a month ago, I'd never had a serious boyfriend. We got fake I.D's at seventeen and have been in the party scene for way too long. I think we were exposed to too much too soon. But, I promise, once you find the right guy to be with, all that stuff will no longer be important. I remember thinking that if I spent a Saturday night at home, I was a loser. But now, I'd much rather be home with Callan than having some strange guy I don't know grinding against me in a crowded club."

She offers up a small smile. "I think about it sometimes. Who knows, maybe Scott will be my Callan."

"I hope so," I agree.

———

AFTER WE EAT, I take Krista back to her apartment to get ready. She talks me into coming up and hanging out with she gets dressed and does her hair and makeup. And since I still haven't heard from Callan, I figure, why not? It's not like I have anything else to do.

She leads me up to her apartment, and I collapse on the couch while she goes into her room to change.

"You can make some coffee if you want. Or there is stuff to drink in the fridge," she tells me from the other room.

I stand up and move to the fridge. I open the door and pull out a bottled iced coffee. I close the fridge and twist the cap, my eyes landing on a picture stuck to the front of the door.

"Is this Scott?" I ask, looking at the picture of her and a guy I don't know. He's cute, with dark hair, blue eyes, and a five o'clock shadow on his chiseled jaw. She's wearing a full-blown smile, causing her blue eyes to shine.

"Yeah, isn't he sexy?"

"He is. Where'd you meet him?" I take a sip of my coffee and head back to the couch.

"At the gallery, actually. He came in and bought a piece. We hit it off immediately, and he left with my number, you know, in case he found himself in need of more art. To my surprise, he called me that night and asked me out." She comes walking into the kitchen in her new black dress and heels.

"Look at you!"

She laughs and spins around. "What do you think?"

"I think you'll leave Scott speechless."

She opens the fridge and pulls out a bottle of water. "Will you come with me? I mean, you don't have to stay long or drink. Just hang out with me until he gets there?"

"I don't know, Kris," I whine, leaning against the counter.

"Please, I don't want to be standing there by myself. You can leave as soon as he gets there."

"Whose party is it?"

"My friend, Gemma's. You've met her a couple of times; remember?"

I nod. "I remember."

She pokes out her bottom lip and gives me her best puppy dog eyes.

"Fine," I breathe out, rolling my eyes. "But I'm not drinking, and I'm leaving as soon as he gets there."

She smiles and jumps up and down. "Thank you, Val," she says, running off to finish getting ready.

CALLAN

I get to work and let myself into Bennet's office. Since it's a Saturday, his secretary isn't at her desk to announce his visitors like usual. I walk in the door and find him sitting behind his desk that's covered in papers.

"Hey," I say, wanting to let him know I'm here.

He doesn't respond. He just keeps his head down, reading over the paperwork.

"Look, man," I start as I walk closer to his desk. He still doesn't look my way.

"Your sister and I, it wasn't planned. I'd never do something like this to you intentionally."

His head pops up. "How did it even begin, Cal? Because last I knew, you wanted to fire her."

I collapse in the seat across from his desk. "It started that weekend she went to the club. Nothing happened between us, but something changed then. Suddenly, she wasn't annoying or trying to ruin my life. When we stopped trying to get at one another, we were able to start a friendship. We found we had a lot of things in common. I just, I got to see her in a different light, I guess. That's when the dreams started. I had these dreams that we were together, like a couple, and I was happy. I can still remember the tingling in my chest from it. Seeing her smile made my heart pound. I told myself no, I did everything I could to get her out of my head, but nothing worked. I knew that I couldn't have the same relationship with her. I kicked her out of my office so I didn't have to look up and see her. I tried being with other women as a way to replace what I really wanted. Nothing worked, and that's why I was going to fire her. I knew that if I couldn't keep my hands to myself, I wouldn't be able to be near her. So I did. I fired her, and then she stormed my house and demanded an answer. All I was trying to do is to get some space to let the feelings pass, but she wouldn't allow space. That's the night everything started."

"Why didn't you tell me?" he asks, seeming to relax a little.

I shrug. "Neither of us even knew what we were doing. At first, we both thought it was a one-time thing, but then it was like we took turns running to each other. I wanted to commit, and she was scared to. I knew it wouldn't be cool with you if we were just fucking around. I wanted to wait until we were in a good place."

"Are you telling me that you and Val, you're in a real relationship?"

I nod. "Neither of us have even looked at anyone else in over a month. She's the one I want, period. I'm going to marry her one day, Ben."

He nods once. "Okay. Hearing all this, it does make it a bit easier to accept, but Cal, I'm still not happy about it. I'm just going to need some time to adjust and accept this. But now, we have to figure out how in the hell to save this account." He shakes his head and begins rubbing his temples.

The doors open and Levi, the company lawyer, walks in. "How the hell did you lose a twenty million-dollar account, Ben?" he asks around a smile.

I raise my hand. "It may have been my fault," I say.

Levi looks at me, smile still in place as he holds out his hand to shake. "Callan, how've you been?"

I shrug and shake his hand. "I've been better, as you can imagine."

He laughs and slips off his jacket. "Move, Ben. Let me look over everything."

Bennet stands up and lets Levi sit down at the desk. "If you can get me out of this one, Levi, you get a bonus," he says around his smile.

Levi winks. "Bennet don't worry, you know there's a clause that protects the company from this kind of reckless behavior. If he doesn't want to take his money out he'll either pay you a very hefty fine or he'll be hit with a lawsuit. Don't worry about it, I'll go through the contract."

Bennet walks over to the drink cart and motions for me to follow him. I stand up and walk across the room, wanting to leave Levi alone so he can figure a way out of this mess.

Bennet pours two drinks and hands me one before we sit in the seating section of his office.

"I'm sorry about all this, man," I tell him, once again.

He waves a hand through the air, dismissing my apologizes. "If that had been Maddie and me, I would've reacted the same way. That's just another reason why you two should've come clean. I mean, do I seem like a total douche to you? I don't understand why you didn't tell me. Were you afraid I'd fire you? Did you think I had the power to make her break up with you?"

I laugh. "Honestly, I thought you'd kick my ass with them boxing skills. Then run me over with a race car."

He laughs but remembers we need to be quiet for Levi to concentrate. He takes a sip of his drink. "It's kind of cool, actually. I mean, if you two are as committed as you say you are. It'd be nice to have my best friend as a brother in law."

I sit up, resting my elbows on my knees as I hold my glass with two hands. "I'm dead serious, Ben. She's it for me."

He smiles. "Good, but I'll tell ya the same thing Damon told me when he found out about Maddie and me."

"What's that?"

"You break her heart, I'll kill ya." His green eyes seem to darken, and his smile falls.

I hold out my hand to shake. "It'll never happen," I promise.

That seems to be all we need to break the ice. The rest of the afternoon, we sit back and chat while Levi does his best to get us out of the mess we're in. We talk about him and Maddie, me and Val, and trips we can take as a couple—he even offers to rent the yacht he and Maddie sailed away on for three months.

Looking back now, it seems silly not telling him. While we both had the time of our lives hiding our secret relationship for a month, this seems even better. Now, we can leave the house. We can go to dinner and hold hands, kiss, and dance like a real couple instead of two business partners having a meeting over a meal. I can go to her family functions and don't have to worry about slipping up and saying the wrong thing. Everything just seems like it will be so much easier now.

"Has your mom been told about us yet?" I ask.

He shakes his head. "I talked to her this morning and told her about this account, just so she feels left in the loop. I mean, it's not anyone's fault we're about to lose it. This kid is irresponsible and just wanting money since his dad passed. His dad may have left him a billion dollar estate but the trust has some serious strings attached so he can't touch it at the moment. But, I didn't tell her about you and Val. I figured that would be for you two to do. I don't see her having a problem with it, though. She's always loved you. You know that."

I smile and nod, happy that nobody will be in our way. Now, we can just be together. We're free to fall deeper in love, to get married, have children, do whatever we want with the rest of our lives. It's funny, before Val, I never wanted marriage or kids or anything to do with being a responsible adult. But now, all I want is her, and I'll do anything, give her anything, to keep her at my side.

"Found something," Levi says, interrupting my thoughts.

Bennet stands and practically runs back to his desk. He places one hand flat on the top as he leaves over and reads the documents.

"I knew your dad had to have snuck something in here to prevent losing that much in one quarter."

Bennet looks up at me, eyes wide and brows arched high. "There's a clause. He can only take a quarter of his money every three months until the funds are paid. It'll take him a year to get all the money, and I have a feeling that after the first one or two withdraws, he'll get bored and forget about it completely."

I stand up with a smile. "Excellent."

"Now, it's time to contact his lawyer," Bennet says, picking up the phone.

———

IT TAKES several hours of talking on the phone, but we finally get the message across. The contract we have is ironclad, and there's no getting out of it. For now, Geo is only able to take a quarter of his money, which pacifies Bennet.

When everything is done, the three of us stand and shake hands.

"How about we all go grab some dinner and a drink?" Bennet asks. "On me for all of your hard work on a Saturday."

We all agree and head down the street for some BBQ. We're seated at a table on the quiet side of the restaurant. It seems that half the restaurant is a bar with a live band playing. The other side is an actual restaurant. I slide into the booth and Bennet takes the seat next to me while Levi sits across from us. Before picking up a menu, I send Val a text.

We're done for the night, but Bennet insisted on buying us dinner and drinks. I'll be home soon. I love you.

I slide my phone into my pocket and pick up the menu just as the waitress is heading over.

"What can I get ya'll to drink tonight?" she asks in her Southern drawl.

"I think I'll take an Old Fashioned," I order as I start to check out the menu.

The other two guys place their drink orders, and the waitress walks away to fill them.

"Levi, thank you for helping us out today on such short notice," Bennet says.

Levi waves his hand through the air. "It's not a problem. That's what I'm here for."

"Well, I'm sure you had something better to do on a Saturday night," Bennet says.

"Nah, not really. Me and my buddy, Nick, were just going to order some food, grab some beer, and sit on his couch and watch the game. But I'm not exactly upset that I missed it."

"Hell, that sounds like a good time to me," Bennet replies, bumping my elbow with his. I nod my head in agreement.

"Me and Nick, we haven't been in the same place lately. He's really changing and getting on my nerves. The only reason he even invited me is because I've been dodging him lately."

Bennet looks over at me. "Sounds like us recently, huh?"

The waitress comes back with our drinks, and I don't waste any time in picking mine up and swallowing down a gulp.

Levi laughs and takes a swig of his drink. "What's going on with you two? Haven't you been like best friends since childhood?"

I pick up my drink. "I've been dating his little sister behind his back," I say, wanting to admit it before he can call me out.

"Oh," Levi says, eyes widening with surprise.

Bennet smiles and nods. "Yeah, nice, huh?" He takes a drink. "So, what's going on with you and Nick?"

Levi suddenly looks nervous as he puts all of his attention on the glass between his two hands. "Honestly, I don't even know. He got this job on Wall Street, and he's just been slowly changing for months now. He used to be cool and laid back, but now all he cares about is money and his social status. His girlfriend, Danielle, she's beautiful and amazing—they've been together for years—he's suddenly treating her like shit. And now, it's at the point where I feel like she's my friend too, and I hate watching her get talked down to by him. It pisses me off just having to be around them," he confesses.

"You got a thing for this girl, don't ya?" I ask, already picking up on the issue.

He shakes his head. "No, it's not like that. She's just been around for years, and I've grown to like her as a friend. I mean, if you have a friend that's a girl, and you had to sit and watch as her boyfriend called her names and cheated on her, how would you feel?"

I hold up my hands, showing him my palms. "Hey, I'm right there with you. I just think it's bothering you as much as it is because you secretly have a thing for her. And either way, you're fucked. You steal her away, you have to deal with him. If you wait for them to break up, and then you two get together, that's a problem too. Bro code and all." I laugh.

He nods and opens his mouth to say something else, but the waitress is back and ready to take our order.

Levi and Bennet start placing their order, and I pull out my phone to see that Val still hasn't texted me back. Again, I type out another message.

Hey, are you okay? Are you mad at me for being out so late? I'm sorry, it wasn't planned. Please, answer me.

I set the phone down on the table next to me so I'll see it light up when she replies.

"How about you, dear?" the waitress asks me.

"I'll take a BBQ sandwich with honey-buffalo sauce, some baked beans, slaw, and onion rings."

We all put our menus away, and the two other guys carry on with their conversations, but I'm too distracted by my phone and wondering why Val hasn't answered me.

17

VALERIE

K rista and I get in my car and she gives me directions to the party. The house is outside of the city, in the suburbs, which means the traffic leaving the city will probably hold us up a good hour —something completely fine by me because I'm not exactly in a hurry to get to a party I'd rather not go to. On the ride, we sit in the car and talk about nothing. We listen to music and sing along with the radio. Finally, there's a break in traffic, and she directs me the rest of the way. I pull onto the road the house is on, and cars are lined up and down the side street. We have to walk almost a block, but finally the house comes into view. I know which one it is based on the crowd on the lawn along with the mix of red plastic cups littering the bushes.

My feet stop walking on their own. "I don't know about this, Kris. I mean, this party looks a little wild."

She grabs my wrist and pulls me forward. "It's not wild. We can't hear the music from here, and there's no sign of people fucking on the lawn. This is one of the more mellow parties we've gone to. Come on." She wraps her arm around my shoulders, keeping me close to her side.

It feels like the second we step onto the lawn, everyone is looking at us.

"Come on, let's go inside," Kris says, releasing me.

I follow along behind her, up across the lawn, up the front porch, and into the house.

"Hey, baby," some guy says as we walk past, but I don't turn around or acknowledge him in any way.

Walking into the house, the loud techno music fills my ears, and it causes my heart to start pounding. Every inch of the place is crowded with people dancing, couples making out, or groups standing around talking and drinking. She leads me through the entryway, into the dining room, and kitchen, and out to the fenced-in backyard. There's a massive pool that has people swimming in it, kegs all along the fence, and the pool house has smoke escaping the windows and doors.

"There's Gemma," Kris says, rushing to a woman that's wearing nothing but a white bikini and heels. She's surrounded by good-looking men, and her hair and makeup are done to perfection. It's easy to tell that she isn't dressed this way to swim. She's just looking for attention.

Kris quickly gives her a hug, and they catch up while I stand back with my arms crossed. I don't know why, but I feel awkward—it's like this is my first party.

"I brought Valerie with me," Kris says, turning to look over her shoulder at me.

I smile and wave.

"What are you doing back there? Come say hi," Kris yells.

I close the distance between us and shake her hand. "How are you?" I ask to be polite.

She smiles. "Really good. Thanks for coming. There's alcohol all over this house. Help yourself."

"Thanks, but I don't drink. I was just bringing Kris, and she talked me into coming in for a sec."

"You're more than welcome to stay. The more the merrier...until the cops get called anyway," she laughs out.

I force a smile and nod my head.

"Let's go find me a drink," Kris says, wrapping her hand around the crook of my arm and leading me off to a keg.

We wait in line until she's handed a red cup, then we take a seat at a patio table.

"Have you seen Scott yet?" I ask, praying that she has so I can get out of here.

She shakes her head and takes a drink. "Not yet. You'll just have to hang out a little bit longer." She smiles wide, causing me to roll my eyes.

We sit and talk while watching everyone at the party do ridiculous things like keg stands. They jump in the pool, play beer pong, and play flip cup. After a couple hours of this, the party gets even crazier. People are now making out and dry humping one another in the outdoor lounge chairs, the music goes from loud to louder, and everyone is stumbling into things, slurring their words, fighting, crying, or puking. Finally, I've had enough.

"Sorry, Kris. But I have to go. Callan will be getting home soon, and we have plans of our own." I quickly stand up.

Her smile falls. "Really? Already? It's not even ten yet," she complains.

I shake my head. "I'm sorry, but this doesn't do it for me. I don't like drinking or partying anymore. And I can't get it out of my head that someone is watching me. I've felt it all night. The hairs on the back of my neck haven't laid down since we walked in here."

She holds out her arms for a hug.

"Do you want a ride home?" I ask, hugging her.

She shakes her head. "Scott will be here soon, and if not, I'll crash with Gemma. But thanks for hanging out with me though."

I smile as I pull away. "Of course."

"Do you want me to walk you out?" she asks, standing up but falling back into her seat.

"No, please don't move...for the rest of the night. I don't want your drunk ass falling into the pool and drowning," I joke.

She laughs. "Call me tomorrow."

"I will," I promise, smiling and waving as I turn around to leave.

Walking out of the house, I take the same route. I walk through the kitchen, dining room, entryway, and out the front door, where there's a ton of people drinking on the porch and lawn.

"There she is. I was wondering when I'd be seeing you again," a guy says as I walk down the steps.

Again, I ignore him and keep walking. I take my keys from my pocket and realize that I left my cell in my car. I wrap my arms around myself as I push myself down the sidewalk as quickly as possible. The further away from the house I get, the darker the street gets, and the quieter the night becomes. Before I can reach my car, I can no longer hear the party, and my racing heart begins to calm, but the hairs on my neck still aren't laying down.

I hear the sound of a twig snapping, and I inhale quickly as I spin around to see where the noise came from. I see nothing but grass, trees, and shrubbery. A long breath leaves me, and I shake my head at myself.

"Get a grip," I whisper, turning back around. But I bump into something hard, causing myself to stumble backward several steps.

I open my mouth to scream, but someone covers it. My eyes focus, and I find Decon holding me with one hand while using the other to cover my mouth. My eyes grow wide with fear, and I try pushing him away, but he's too strong.

"Shhhh, Val," he whispers as he pulls me closer to him. I fight and thrash, kicking my arms and legs, trying to get away, but his hold doesn't break.

"Stop fucking around, Val," he says low in my ear. "Don't make me fucking hurt you."

But his words don't calm the panic that's being pumped throughout my body. Instead, it only fuels it to go faster as I notice he's urging me toward a car that's not mine. He opens the trunk, and it makes me fight even harder. I jab my elbow into his stomach, and he lets out a growl.

"You fucking asked for this," he says, using something to strike me on top of the head.

My ears ring, my eyes blur and start turning black around the edges; pain washes over me as something hot runs down my face. The blackness takes over, and I lose consciousness.

———

MY HEAD IS POUNDING. I know I need to open my eyes, but I don't want the light to make it hurt worse. I try to roll myself into a ball, but my hands are above my head, and they're not moving. Then, the memories hit me. Leaving the party, being alone, Decon.

My eyes pop open, and I find myself alone in a bedroom. My hands are tied to the headboard above my head. I pull against the zip tie, but it doesn't budge. Tears flood my eyes as I look around me, trying to figure out where I am. It's clearly a guy's bedroom. There are clothes everywhere: on the floor beside the bed, hanging on the footboard, piling up on a chair in the corner. The walls are covered in artwork, everything from posters of classic paintings to new, modern stuff you can buy at the gallery I used to work at. There's a small bedside lamp on the table next to the bed, and it lights up the room enough for me to see. I see a familiar Cubs hat hanging from the post on the footboard—it's old, dirty, and worn. Immediately, I know I'm in Decon's bedroom.

Fuck. What is he going to do with me? Why now? If he was going to come after me, why did he wait so long? Why didn't he do this after that night?

I want to yell for help, but my instincts tell me not to. Instead, I look around me in hopes of finding something I can use to cut the zip tie off my wrists. While my eyes scan the area around me for scissors or a knife, I listen, hearing small thumps and taps from outside of the room.

"What the fuck is the plan, Decon?" someone whisper yells.

"I don't know. I panicked," Decon says. "I didn't plan this."

"I'm not going to be a part of this. Get her out of here." The door slams, causing me to jump.

Seconds later, the bedroom door opens, and Decon walks in. His eyes land on mine and he freezes.

"What are you doing with me?" I ask, voice strained.

He shakes his head as he walks into the room and closes the door behind him. "This is all your fault. You know that?"

"My fault?" I ask, surprise evident in my voice.

"All you had to do was leave me the fuck alone. But you couldn't do that, could you? You had to fucking tease me and make me think you liked me, that you wanted me."

"Decon, I—"

"No, you don't get to talk now. You don't even know all the trouble you've stirred up for me, do you?" He's towering over me, anger contorting his features.

I open my mouth, but no words come out as I shake my head.

"It didn't make sense at first. Until I saw you at Hanger 10. You danced with one guy, then nearly got him beat up by another two guys. You're playing all of them, aren't you?"

I shake my head no.

"Bull shit! You're playing them like you played me." He reaches out and his palm lands hard across my face.

Tears sting my eyes, but I refuse to let them fall. All he wants is to see me hurt. I won't give him the satisfaction. "Bennet is my brother!"

"Who's the other guy? The guy that came up in here and beat my ass? The guy you left with last night?" He bends down so close that I can smell the alcohol on his breath.

I shake my head, refusing to tell him a name.

He reaches out, and his hand wraps around my throat. He squeezes, not enough to stop my air supply, but enough to let me know he's serious. "Who is he?"

"He's my boyfriend," I croak out.

He releases me. "He's the one that has me being followed. He's the one that came in here and stole from me. What's his name?" he asks, bending back down.

"Followed by who?" I ask, confused. I didn't know Callan knew anything about Decon.

"The police. He fucking tipped them off. I can't go anywhere without seeing them watch me. Now, what's his name?"

"What are you going to do?" I ask, pulling against the restraints.

"I'm going to make him pay. Make him pay for what he took from me; make him pay for stealing you." He climbs onto the bed, straddling me. "Tell me his name, Valerie."

"No. He didn't steal me. I was never yours. I've always been his. He didn't have to drug me to get me into his bed. That's more than I can say about you!" I spit out.

Something inside of him snaps, and he lets out this guttural yell as he reaches out and cups his hands around my neck, squeezing hard. I fight against him even though I can't get air to my lungs. I wiggle and kick, trying to knock him off of me any way I can. But then, something flashes in his eyes and his lips turn up into a grin as his hands begin to go loose.

He licks his lips as his eyes move up and down, taking me in. "I guess if you're not going to give me what I want, I'll take what should've been mine all along." His hands release my throat, but then move down to the neck of my shirt, pulling in opposite directions until I hear the fabric tear and the cold air kiss my skin.

It's now when I realize that he's going to do something worse than kill me. He's going to torture me. This one moment will forever be trapped in the back of my head, tormenting me for the rest of my life. I buck my hips upward and trash around while the screams that have been stuck in my throat finally come out.

His hand covers my mouth while the other digs in his pocket for something else: a knife. He pulls it out and flicks it open, showing me the blade. It catches the light, and it gleams.

"Stop. Be quiet. Do you hear me?" he asks, placing the blade to my throat.

The tears finally build up and fall over the rims of my eyes as I nod my head. He drags the blunt end of the knife down my chest and between my breasts. Quickly, he pulls it back up, cutting through the center of my bra. It pops open, and my breasts bounce free.

18

CALLAN

Dinner runs longer than I'd like, and the whole time, I can't stop staring at my phone. Finally, Bennet pays the check, and we get up to leave. We all walk out together, and Levi says goodbye before climbing behind the wheel of his car. I rush toward mine, but Bennet follows along behind me.

"Cal, what's up?"

I shake my head as I slide into the driver's seat. "Val's not answering her phone."

He shrugs. "So, it's going on ten? She's probably in bed, or out with that no good best friend of hers."

I shake my head. "No, she hasn't been hanging out with her. And I don't think she'd go to bed without me. We had plans."

"You think she's in trouble?" he asks, brows pulling together.

"I don't know, but I'm going to find out."

"I'll follow you," Bennet says, rushing to his car.

I slam my door closed and put the keys into the ignition. The car roars to life when I twist the key. I hurriedly shift into drive and hit the gas. I weave in and out of traffic, hitting the highway. Silently, I pray that I don't hit traffic. On the drive, I call her phone over and over, but every time, it goes to voicemail. I know she isn't sleeping. No way could she sleep through a constantly ringing phone at her side.

I drive like a crazy person, going around people on the shoulder of the road at ninety miles per hour. Finally, I see my exit, and I shoot onto it. I blow through stoplights and signs with only a quick pause to make sure it's clear. Twenty minutes after leaving the restaurant, I'm pulling up to my house.

Immediately, I realize that her car isn't in the drive. I throw the car into park and shut it off as I'm stepping out. I'm walking in the front door when Bennet's headlights shine into the driveway. I run through the downstairs, only finding dark rooms. Finally, I rush upstairs and into our bedroom. The room is dark, but when I flip the light on, hoping to find her asleep in my bed, all I find is a piece of paper. I pick it up and read over it.

Callan,

I'm going to spend the day with Kris. We're going to get lunch and then hit the mall to find her a dress for some party tonight. Be home later.

Love you,
Val

I crumble it up and toss it over my shoulder as I turn for the door, bumping into Bennet.

"She's not here?" he asks.

I shake my head. "She's with Kris. You got her number?"

He nods. "I think so." He pulls his phone from his pocket and starts searching through his contacts. "Yeah, here it is." He hits the call button and brings the phone to his ear. He holds it there for what feels like forever before she answers.

He pulls it away and puts it on speaker.

"Helllllllo?" she slurs into the phone.

"Kris, it's Callan. Is Valerie with you?"

"No, she took off a while ago. She isn't home yet?"

"No, where are you?"

"I'm at a party in the suburbs," she answers, sounding drunker than when she answered the phone.

"Give me the address," I demand.

She rattles off the address and Bennet and I rush toward the door.

A little while later, we're pulling into a crowded street. "There! That's her car," I say, pointing at it. Bennet quickly stops, and I jump out, rushing over to it and looking in the window. The car is empty. Again, I pull out my phone and call her. A light shines from inside the car, and I peek in the window to see her phone sitting in the cupholder in the center.

"Fuck!" I kick the tire just as Bennet comes rushing up. "I found her phone. She must still be here somewhere."

"Come on. Let's ask around," Bennet says.

We walk across the street and onto the sidewalk. My heart is pounding, and my nerves are shot. The street is dark, but I can see a hint of something sparkling off in the distance. I quickly walk up to it. Bending down, I find a set of keys. I grab them and lift them to see them more clearly.

"They're hers," I mumble.

"How do you know?' Bennet asks.

"Because I gave her this keychain last week," I say, holding up the heart-shaped keychain.

"Come on. Maybe she realized she lost her keys on the way in and she's looking for them," Bennet says, walking forward.

We walk through the party and search every room. We ask everyone we can if they've seen her. I even pull up a picture of her to show them, but they all say no, they don't know her or haven't seen her here tonight.

"Fuck, where could she be?" I ask, getting anxious, pissed, and worried.

"Maybe she got a ride home to Mom's," Bennet says, stepping off to the side and pulling out his phone.

"Mom? Is Valerie there?" he asks.

His eyes meet mine, and he shakes his head. "Alright, Mom. Thanks." He hangs up and slides the phone back into his pocket.

"Let's try somewhere else," I say, refusing to give up.

We walk back through the house and out the front door when I think to ask the guys hanging out front.

"Hey, have you seen this woman?" I ask, showing him a picture of her on my phone.

He nods. "Yeah, I tried talking to her tonight, but she blew me off."

"Do you know where she went or even what direction she went in last?"

He nods toward the street. "I think she was leaving. She walked out of the yard and took a right on the sidewalk."

"Was anyone following her, or did someone leave after her going in the same direction?" Bennet asks.

The guy stops and thinks for a moment. "Now that you mention it, yeah. She left, and it wasn't a minute later that a guy walked out of the side of the fence and went the same way."

"Do you know who it was?" I ask.

"Nah, I never saw him before."

"What did he look like?"

He takes a drink and leans sits on the porch railing. "I'd say he's about my height, but a little bigger. He had dark hair, and he was wearing a dirty Cubs hat. I didn't really get a good look at his face. It's dark, you know?"

Bennet looks at me. "Does any of that sound familiar?"

I nod but think it's a long shot. "Thanks, man." I slide my phone back into my pocket and take off running toward the car with Bennet following along behind me.

"Hey, where are you going? Do you know who that guy is? Damnit, Callan. Tell me something."

"I think it's the guy that attacked her at the club that night."

"What? Why would it be him?" he asks, climbing behind the wheel.

"This guy was pissed that she wouldn't sleep with him. I guess they'd been hanging out, flirting and kissing for months. She always left him hanging, though."

"Okay, that explains why he tried drugging her, but why would he abduct her?"

"I tracked him down and beat the shit out of him. I took his drugs in hopes of saving another girl. I also tipped off the police. I said he's attacking women and selling drugs to kids."

"So you think he's taken her as a way to get back at you?"

I shrug. "I have no idea, but it's worth a shot."

Bennet's grip on the steering wheel tightens, and his foot gets a little heavier as he steps on the gas, throwing me back in my seat. "What's the address?"

I rattle off the address and tell him ahead of time when he needs to turn. Since his apartment is in the rougher part of Chicago, it takes us a while to get there with all the late-night, Saturday traffic.

We pull up to the apartment building a little while later, and Bennet shuts off the car.

"What's the plan?"

"We storm in there and search the place."

"And if she's not in there?" he asks.

"If she's not in there, I'll beat the shit out of him again and demand he give us some answers."

"You know this is a home invasion, right? We could get in big trouble for this."

"It's worth the risk," I tell him, opening my door and stepping out.

I lead him up to his apartment, and just as I'm about to kick the door in, Bennet places his arm across my chest, holding me back.

"What the fuck, man?" I whisper.

"Just stop and listen for a second." He places his ear to the door to listen for any sounds.

I stand there, bouncing from one foot to the other, adrenaline pumping through my body. Every muscle in my body is tensed and ready to go, to break down this fucking door and turn everything upside down until I find her.

I hear a shriek from inside the apartment, and I push Bennet aside as I ram my shoulder into the door. The wood pops and cracks, but it flies open. It bounces off the wall with a loud bang.

"Call the police," I tell Bennet, rushing through the apartment. I walk through the living room and into the hallway. I hear some banging from inside the room in front of me, and I slowly open the door. On the other side I find Decon, back against the furthest wall. He has Valerie against his chest, facing me as he holds a knife to her throat. It feels like time freezes. All I can do is look at her. Her dark hair is matted with blood, and it's been running onto her forehead where it dried. Her face is red like he's smacked her. Her lip is busted and bruising, and her eye is black and swollen. She's completely topless, and he's stripped her of her pants, leaving her in just a pair of panties. Her entire body is either red or bruised, and she has tiny nicks and cuts that are dripping a small amount of blood. It's easy to see what his plan was here.

"Don't fucking move or I'll slit her throat," he spits out.

Valerie whimpers as tears fall down her cheeks.

"Let her go," I demand. "Let her go, and we'll walk out of here right now. No cops. No trouble. Just let her go."

He laughs. "The cops are already here. They've been parked outside for weeks now. I didn't make sense of it until I saw you guys together last night. Then, everything clicked: why you came here, why the cops were suddenly everywhere I went. You fucked up my life. It's time I fucked up yours." He pulls the knife away from her throat but jabs it in her side. She lets out a scream that pierces my ears. I rush forward, and he pushes her into my arms as he runs toward the door. But I don't bother to chase him because I know Bennet's there and he's never getting out.

I lay her down on the bed and grab a sheet to ball up.

"I'm so sorry, Val, but this is going to hurt." I quickly kiss her on the head before applying pressure to her side with the balled-up sheet. She lets out a moan and her body tenses.

"I know you're in pain but stay with me. Keep your eyes open. Focus on me." I dig my phone out of my pocket and call 9-1-1.

"9-1-1, what's your emergency?"

"My girlfriend has been stabbed. I need an ambulance," I tell them, rattling off the address. I don't listen to what she has to say. I can't. I can only focus on Valerie. The way her skin is growing paler by the moment, the way her eyes seems to glaze over, the way her breathing becomes shallow and slower.

"Stay awake, Val. Look at me," I cry out, placing my fingers on the inside of her wrist to check her pulse. It's weak, but it's there.

Bennet rushes into the room. "I caught him and knocked him out. I found a zip tie and I tied him up," he says before his eyes land on Valerie laying lifeless, bruised, and bleeding.

"Go outside and direct the EMTs," I order, but he doesn't move. He's frozen, eyes locked on his sister's beat-up body.

"Go!" I yell, snapping him out of it. He nods, turns, and runs for the door.

It feels like hours go by, but it's only minutes before the EMTs are rushing into the room. They check her over quickly and load her up onto the gurney. As I'm walking out to follow them to the hospital, the police walk in and cuff Decon.

One of them looks up at me. "Did you have probable cause to enter this residence?"

I nod. "I heard her scream."

They both nod and lift a bloodied Decon from the floor. I guess Bennet took a couple hits for himself.

"We'll have a few questions for you later, but right now, you can go to the hospital."

Bennet and I follow the ambulance to the hospital, but we're told to wait in the waiting room while she's examined. Bennet calls Maddie and his mother while I pace back and forth.

I'm so engrossed in my thoughts and worries that I don't notice him leave, but he comes back and hands me a coffee.

A nurse walks up. "Are you the family of Valerie Windsor?"

"Yes!" we both jump to say.

"We're moving her into surgery now due to internal bleeding. I'll update you when we know more." She rushes back through the swinging doors before either of us can ask any questions. We both collapse into the chairs, neither of us talking. I think we're both in shock at tonight's turn of events. We're both sick with worry, anger, and sadness.

Maddie and Valerie's mom both rush into the ER waiting area and up to Bennet. He explains what happened and how they've moved Val into surgery. Everyone is now panicked, anxious, and worried.

I slide back into my seat and lean my head against the wall while my eyes drift closed. All I see is her. Her smile; her shining green eyes. I can feel her soft skin against mine. I can smell her sweet scent. I can taste heavenly lips against mine. I pray that she'll be okay, that she'll return to me.

19

VALERIE

I hear a soft beeping sound. It goes on and on, never stopping. My body is flooded with pain, and all I want to do is give in to it, let it pull me back under so I no longer have to feel it. But that damn beeping sound keeps growing louder and louder. My eyes flutter open, and I find myself in a hospital bed. I let out a sigh, happy to see that I'm out of Decon's and still alive. I turn my head and find Callan, asleep at my side.

"Callan," I say softly, unable to make my voice any louder. My throat is dry and sore. It feels like I've had a red-hot branding iron shoved down it. "Callan," I say again, a bit louder.

He jumps awake, and his eyes lock on mine. His mouth drops open as he moves closer to me. He picks up my hand and gently squeezes it as he falls to his knees beside my bed. "You're okay, Val. Everything is going to be okay," he tells me, over and over. I'm not sure if it's for my benefit or if he's trying to convince himself.

I nod. "Drink?" I motion toward my throat.

"Of course," he says, getting up and grabbing a Styrofoam cup with a lid and a straw. He holds it to my lips and allows me to swallow down a big gulp of water that burns my throat even more, but it's cold and wet, so it relieves the pain I feel.

"They said your throat might be sore after the surgery from the endotracheal tube."

"Where's the doctor?" I ask, trying to get myself pushed up in bed.

He places his hand on mine. "Don't move. You don't want to rip open your stitches. I'll get him; just don't move." His eyes are wide and serious as he turns and runs from the room.

I nod and stop trying to get myself up.

Moments later, Callan and a doctor walk into my room.

"How are you feeling, Valerie?" the doctor asks as Callan kneels back at my side. I don't know how long I've been here, but I'm starting to wonder if he's left my side at all.

I nod. "I've felt better," I admit.

He chuckles but grabs the chart at the foot of the bed. "I'm sure you have. It appears that you will be fine. You had some internal bleeding from the stab wound, but everything has been cauterized and stitched up. We're going to keep you on fluids and antibiotics for a couple of days. We don't want you getting an infection, and you were rather dehydrated. All you need is time, and you'll be as good as new."

"Thank you, doctor."

His eyes scan the chart one last time. "Oh, and it appears the baby is fine and healthy."

"The what?" Callan and I both ask at the same time.

The doctor seems surprised by our confusion. "Yes, it shows here that you are about eight weeks pregnant. You didn't know?" he asks with a raise of his brow.

We both shake our heads, but I think back eight weeks. That must have been our first weekend together, the time that we both woke in the middle of the night only to have unprotected sex and go back to sleep.

"I'm...we're...?" I stutter, unable to form words due to shock.

The doctor nods. "That's right. You're going to be parents. Congratulations." He smiles wide before setting the chart down and leaving the room.

I look up at Callan, and he looks down at me. "Did you know about this?" he asks.

I shake my head. "I had no idea. I mean, I've been on birth control since I was fifteen."

"You didn't miss a period?" he asks, sitting on the edge of my bed.

"My periods have never been regular. It's completely normal for me to go two or three months without having one at all."

We both grow quiet as we think about the information we were just given.

"How do you feel? What do you think?" I ask Callan when he doesn't speak up.

He falls back onto his knees as he picks up my hand and presses a kiss to the top. "I'm just glad you're okay. I was so scared that I was going to lose you." His blue eyes begin to fill with tears.

I smile. "I'm fine, but what do you think about being a father? We never talked about it before."

He smiles wide. "I already knew I wanted to be with you for the rest of my life. Having a baby, it just makes everything better." He stands up and pulls me in for a long, slow kiss.

The door opens, and he pulls away to see Bennet, Maddie, and my mom come walking in. They all rush to my bed, gathering around me.

"Are you okay?" Maddie asks.

"Honey, how are you feeling?" Mom asks.

"I'm fine. Sore and tired but fine," I assure them.

"Should we tell them the good news?" Callan asks from behind them. He walks around the bed and stands at my side.

I look at my mom. "Mom, Callan and I have been carrying on a relationship for a couple of months now."

Her mouth drops open, and the corners turn up into a smile. "Oh, well that's wonderful, honey."

I nod. "And we just found out that I'm pregnant."

Everyone gasps and smiles and talks all at once—all of them equally excited.

Hours pass, and everyone stays by my side until the sun goes down. Finally, Maddie and Bennet offer to take my mom home for the night. Callan shuts the door and pulls a chair up next to me. He holds my hand as he sits down.

"You've had a busy day. You need to get some rest." He presses his lips to my hand.

I smile. "I can't wait to get out of here and back home with you. I want you to lay with me, hold me."

"That we can fix," he says, climbing next to me in bed. I curl into his side with his arm beneath my neck. I roll to my good side, my hurt side facing the ceiling.

"Was Decon arrested?" I just now think to ask.

"He was. And I don't think he'll be released any time soon. He has charges against him for abduction, assault, bodily harm and endangerment, and attempted rape. The police also found drugs. He won't bother you again," he promises.

"I can't believe this. It's all so mind-blowing. I mean, I've known Decon for a year. I guess it goes to show you how little you can know about a person."

"Everyone shows their true colors eventually," he mumbles, pressing his lips to my forehead.

I take a deep breath and breathe him in, letting his familiar scent soothe and relax me into a deep, dreamless sleep.

A couple days pass, and I'm finally allowed to go home. While I'm still stiff and sore and in pain, I couldn't be happier to get out of the hospital. Callan has stayed by my side the entire time, and I think we could both use some rest and relaxation—something you can't get in a hospital. He drives me back to his place and helps me inside. He carries me up to his room and places me in bed gently. He sits at the foot of the bed and begins removing my shoes and jeans. When I'm in nothing but a loose-fitting shirt, he strips himself and crawls up beside me. His hot skin touches mine, and it feels like he's burned me. It's funny how even in pain, a simple touch from him has me begging for more.

I cup his jaw and he rolls to his side, giving me a long, slow, soft kiss. He pulls away, and something in his eyes changes. "Don't do this to me, Val," he pleads.

"Do what?" I ask.

"I see that look in your eyes. We can't. You're hurt." I giggle but stop quickly because of the pain in my side. "I need you, Callan. I thought I'd never get to touch you again."

He presses a kiss to my forehead. "No, Valerie. I love you, and I want you just as badly as you want me, but I won't hurt you. You need to take it easy and rest. Are you hungry? I'll get you something." Without a reply, he stands from the bed and rushes out the door.

Even though I'm annoyed at being turned down, I smile at how much he loves and cares for me.

He comes back several long minutes later, and he has a bag full of stuff and a breakfast tray. He sits the tray over my lap, and there's a bowl of soup, a grilled cheese, a piece of chocolate cake, and a glass of iced tea. He begins unloading the bag that holds soda, water, magazines, books, and a coloring book and crayons.

I laugh as I pick up my chocolate cake and begin eating it. "Don't want to get back out of bed today?" I ask.

"This way, you'll have everything you need without having to ask." He comes back around the bed to lay back beside me.

"What about a toilet?" I joke.

He shrugs. "I'll just carry you to it."

I shake my head. "I think I can walk, Callan. You don't have to do all of this." I hold out my fork that has a bite of cake on the end.

He takes it and swallows it down. "Yes, I do. I'm staying right here, by your side, until you get cleared by the doctor. I've already talked to Bennet about taking medical leave."

"You can't do that, Callan."

"I can, and I did. So don't even try to argue. Oh yeah, and Bennet and Maddie picked up your car and brought it home while you were in the hospital."

"I can't believe I forgot about my car." I put down the empty plate and lay my head back.

"Krista is supposed to come visit you too. I think she feels a little guilty."

"Guilty about what?" I ask, confused.

"She said she had to talk you into going to that party. If she wouldn't have done that, you wouldn't have been there, and you would've been fine."

I nod. That does sound like Krista. "It's not her fault. Actually, it's probably a good thing it happened the way it did. I mean, Decon is off the street now. He can't come for me or any other girl for a long time. There's no telling how many women we saved."

He kisses the top of my hand. "I'm sure you're right, but I wish you didn't have to get hurt in all of this."

I wave him off. "Want some of my grilled cheese and tomato soup?"

He smiles and props his head up with his fist, where I feed him after taking a bite myself.

Hours pass, and the sun begins to fade. I'm wide awake, unable to sleep because I've done nothing but lay around and sleep for what feels like a week. But what I am able to do is watch Callan sleep beside me.

His blond hair is pushed back away from his face, and his blue eyes are shut. His blond eyelashes are fanned out on his cheeks, and he has a scruffy five o'clock shadow growing on his jaw. It's easy to see how much stress he's been under these last few days, but while he sleeps, it all fades away. He looks so relaxed and worry-free. His hard chest is rising and falling slowly with his deep, even breathing, and his basketball shorts are low on his hips. Even though he's dead asleep, his hard six-pack is still visible, and every second I stare at it, it only teases me more. I want to run my fingers across them, feel them as they tense and ease.

I reach out and place my hand on his stomach, and they instantly tighten with my touch. His breathing gets louder and more rushed.

I can't help myself as my hand descends lower, beneath the waistband of his shorts. My hand wraps around his growing erection, and I slowly pump him up and down. He lets out a soft moan and my eyes jump up to his, but he still seems like he's asleep. Maybe he thinks this is a dream.

I push myself to keep going, gaining speed with each pump.

Finally, he lets out a moan, and his eyes pop open just as warm stickiness spills out over my hand. He's breathing heavy as his eyes lock on mine.

"You've been a very naughty girl, Valerie," he says, trying to remain serious, but I can see the grin he's holding back.

He sits up and urges me back until I'm lying flat on the bed. He crawls between my knees, gently pulling my panties down my thighs.

"I'm going to punish you for that one," he says, lowering his mouth to my clit, making me see stars with one sweep of his tongue.

20

CALLAN

ONE MONTH LATER...

"WHAT'S the first thing you want to do now that you've been cleared by the doctor?" I ask her as I slide behind the wheel.

She grins. "I bet you can guess." Her grin turns into a coy smile.

I shake my head. "Are you serious?"

"We haven't had sex in a month, Callan. You'd think you'd want it worse than I do."

"Oh, I do," I agree, sliding the keys into the ignition. "But, after you assaulted me in my sleep, it's not like you haven't gotten off at all. I've been a slave to your body for weeks now."

She giggles. "I loved every second of the touches and kisses that have pushed me over the edge, but I want you back inside me where you're meant to be." She pulls her seatbelt across her chest. "Take me home, Callan."

"Yes, ma'am," I agree, shifting into drive and leaving the doctor's office parking lot.

As I drive us home, her hand is resting on my dick. Every once in a while, she'll move it up and down, and for kicks, she adds in a nice squeeze. Needless to say, by the time we make it home, I'm painfully hard.

I slam on the brakes, shift into park, and pull out the keys as I step out onto the concrete. I practically run around the car, opening her door and pulling her out into my arms. Her mouth lands on mine as her arms wrap around my neck. I pick her up against me, walking us inside without breaking our kiss. I press her back to the front door while my hands travel her body. She begins pushing my shirt up my chest but freezes when we hear a loud, "Surprise!"

My mouth stops, as does hers. She slides down my body, and we both turn, awkwardly, to face the people that are now crowded up behind us. My eyes take them in: Bennet, Maddie, Jazz, Damon, Krista, and Val's Mom, who's holding a cake.

"What is all this?" Val asks, pushing her shirt back down her stomach.

"It's your surprise baby shower," Kris says.

"But we don't even know the sex of the baby yet," Val says, face growing redder and redder.

Maddie laughs. "And it's a party to celebrate getting back on your feet. Callan told Bennet that the doctor has released you for work. That's great news!"

My eyes flash over to Bennet, who's hiding his smile behind his fist. "Thanks, man. This couldn't have waited a few hours?"

Everyone begins to head out to the back patio. He shrugs. "I can honestly say I never considered you'd be hopping into bed the moment you got home."

"I haven't been able to touch my girlfriend in a month," I point out.

He laughs. "Ouch."

"Yeah," I agree.

"Well, you've waited a month; what's a couple more hours?" he asks, slapping me on the back and leading me into my office where he knows the good drinks are.

He pours us both a drink and Maddie walks in. "I knew I'd find the good stuff in here. The only thing out there is sparkling cider." She picks up a glass and holds it out for Bennet to pour her some.

"So, Mads. When are you two having kids?" I ask, taking a sip and sitting down on the leather sofa.

Maddie's eyes grow wide, and she nearly chokes on her drink. "Never," she coughs out.

"What? Why?" I ask, leaning forward to rest my elbows on my knees.

She rolls her eyes. "Ask me that question again in six months." She laughs before walking out and leaving us alone.

Bennet walks over and sits at my side. "Cal, I have something for you." He reaches into his pocket and pulls out a small box.

"I'm sorry, man. But I can't marry you," I joke.

"Haha, fucker," he says, handing me the box. "It's my Mom's wedding ring. She gave me my grandma's for when Maddie and I got married, but this one was hers. She wants Val to have it, but that doesn't mean you have to ask her to marry you. Or maybe you have a family ring of your own you're wanting to use one of these days."

I open the box and see the beautiful ring. It's a massive princess cut diamond set on a gold band. It has dozens of tiny little diamonds surrounding it. I know Val loves it, and it's from her late father.

"Thanks, Ben," I say, still staring at the diamond and wondering if I should ask her to marry me. Somewhere deep inside of me, I've always known we'd be married one day, but I never put much thought into how or when. I just knew we'd get there. Maybe this is a sign. Maybe this is when I'm supposed to ask her. I mean, she's already pregnant with my child and we're in the process of moving her things from her mom's house to mine.

I slide the box into my pocket just as Jazz sticks her head into the room. "Hey, boys. Come on. Val is going to open some gifts, and then we're doing cake."

We both stand and walk out the French doors and onto the patio. "Hey, how'd you get in my house anyway?" I ask.

Bennet laughs. "I had Kris sneak it off of Val's keys. Here it is, by the way." He hands over the key, and I slide it into my pocket.

"That girl scares me sometimes," I say with a laugh.

We sit and watch as Val opens her gifts. She gets things for the baby such as bottles, diapers, pacifiers, and a few clothing items in neutral colors. When everyone sits down with their piece of cake, I drop down to one knee in front of Valerie.

Everyone gets silent as they freeze and watch what I'm doing.

I pick up her hand and hold it in mine. "Valerie," I begin, and immediately, she starts tearing up.

"You know how crazy I am about you," I laugh out. "It's funny, because before you, I never knew what I needed. I didn't even know what I wanted. But then, something with us changed. You went from being the girl that drove me insane to being the girl that made my heart race. From the moment I knew I wanted you, I knew I'd marry you. I knew that we were meant to be, that I'd never survive losing you. So, while I've known for months now that we'd be married one day, I never thought about when or how I'd ask you. Not until five minutes ago when your brother slipped me this little box." I pull the box from my pocket.

"Apparently, this was your mother's ring, a ring your father bought for her to say how much he loved her. She wanted you to have it, but Bennet made it perfectly clear that I didn't have to propose with it. But I got to thinking about you and me and this little baby we're bringing into the world, and thought, this is it. This is the moment I'm supposed to ask you to marry me, to be by my side forever. And even though I didn't spend months trying to plan out the perfect way of asking, I know that this is it. Right now, we're surrounded by everyone we love, and this ring making its way into my hands, it proves it. This is us: fast, thoughtless, but always spot on. I promise to love you every single day for the rest of my life. I promise to cherish you, hold you, take care of you. Valerie, will you please do me the honor of becoming my wife?"

Everyone is dead still while we all watch the emotions on Valerie's face change. She nods and smiles wide. "Yes!"

I slide the ring onto her finger as everyone stands and cheers us on. Finally, I pull her closer and press a kiss to her mouth: a kiss that marks the first day of the rest of our lives together, a day that means we'll never be alone again. A day when we belong to each other.

We enjoy the rest of the party and Bennet and Maddie stick around to help us get everything cleaned up. Finally, we show them to the door.

"Sorry for intruding on your moment earlier," Maddie says, hugging Val.

She waves her hand through the air, dismissing the thought. "No worries. We're going to make up for it now though," she jokes.

I wave goodbye and pull Val back into the house. "Now, where were we?" I ask, backing her up until her back presses to the door. I move my mouth to hers, and it's like we were never interrupted. She wraps her arms around my neck, and I pick her up against me. Her hands find their way up my shirt, and she works it up until I break away to rip it from my body. The second it hits the floor, I'm right back on her, needing to be inside my fiancée.

She lets out a whimper that calls to me like no sound ever has. It causes my dick to twitch against her. It makes me lose my mind, and I can't think of anything but her. My body has missed her this last month. I turn us around and carry her up the stairs, kissing her the whole way. When we get into the bedroom, I set her softly on the bed and crawl up her body. She pulls away her shirt, and my fingers get to work on her bra, setting her free. My eyes zero in on her breasts that are now growing along with her belly that's still mostly flat.

"Please, be gentle. They're so sore I could cry," she whispers.

I pull away and opt to only press light kisses to the skin, avoiding the nipple altogether. I kiss down her ribs and to her stomach where our little baby is growing.

"I love you," I whisper against her stomach.

"I love you too," she says as I pull away and start working her skirt down her legs.

When she's completely stripped and bare before me, I don't bother with lowering my mouth to her clit. That's all we've done for a month, and I know she needs more than that. I place myself at her entrance and thrust forward, filling her to the brim. She lets out a loud moan that tells me I'm right where I need to be.

Her nails dig into my back, pushing me to keep moving, but I'm so lost, I know that if I don't go slow, everything will be over in five minutes. I need her more than that. She needs me. Instead of moving, I kiss her. Long, hard, and deep. I don't move until she's whimpering beneath me and begging me to.

Finally, I slide out of her, only to thrust back in just as deeply as before, but this time, I roll my hips against hers.

———

I WAKE in the morning and I roll to my side, happy to see her sleeping peacefully beside me. Her long, dark lashes are fanned out across her cheeks, and all I can hear is her deep, even breathing. I close my eyes and take a long breath, living in this moment: a moment where everything is perfect, a time that I can just relax and be happy.

When her hand cups my cheek, my eyes pop open, and my lips turn up in a smile. "Good morning," I softly whisper, brushing a stand a hair away from her beautiful face.

She kisses my palm and smiles. "Good morning."

She rolls into my side, and I wrap her up in my arms, holding her close, refusing ever to let go.

"What's on the agenda for today?" she asks, sleepily rubbing her eyes.

"I was thinking, now that your doctor has released you, we could go to your mom's and finish packing. That way, you can live here full time instead of always needing to run back and forth when you need something."

She offers up a weak smile. "Sounds perfect."

"Why don't you get up and take a shower, and I'll go down and get started on some coffee and breakfast." I move to sit up, but she latches onto my arm.

"Wait. Why don't you join me in the shower?" she asks, pulling my mouth to hers.

I laugh around our kiss. "Because then we'll never get out of this house, and I want you here full time, never having an excuse to leave." I stand up and gently smack her ass. "Now, get busy, woman."

She giggles from behind me as I walk out of the room and toward the kitchen.

VALERIE

W atching him walk out of the bedroom in nothing but a pair of boxers has my heart racing. With each rippled muscle, with every sway of his hips, it beats harder and harder and makes me want to pull him back into bed where I can seduce him into never walking away from me again. But a part of me is just as excited for the next step in our relationship as he is. I want to live here with him. I want to get married. I want this little baby that I didn't even know about but love wholeheartedly already. I place my hand on my stomach and look down.

"Your daddy is something else, little one."

I laugh and shake my head at myself. In a way, none of this feels real. I never thought that this would be my life. I never considered working for a large company. I didn't think I'd be ready to settle down at twenty-one with marriage and a kid. But here I am, ready to jump in headfirst. I know some would question my choices, I mean, I am really young. But this is something some people work for their whole lives. I shouldn't run away from it just because I found mine a little sooner than most—most don't have a Callan of their own.

I push all thoughts away as I stand from the bed. The moment my feet hit the floor, I feel dizzy. My mouth begins to water, and my stomach rolls. It growls and feels like I'm about to lose everything inside. I rush to the bathroom and fall to my knees just as I empty my stomach in the toilet. After several long minutes of retching, I wipe the sweat from my brow and flush the toilet.

"Morning sickness at its best," I mumble as I move toward the shower.

I still feel sick and dizzy, my ears are ringing, and for some reason, the smell of eggs hits me, making my stomach flop yet again. I slide down the wall and sit in the shower floor while the hot water pours over me.

The longer I sit here, the better I feel, but then Callan opens the glass shower door, and that smell gets even stronger, making me gag and rush for the toilet again.

He shuts off the water and rushes to my side, pulling my hair behind me. "What's wrong? Are you okay?"

I nod as I gag, having nothing left to throw up. "Morning sickness," I mumble. "The smell of that food is horrible."

"It's just eggs, bacon, and toast."

"I'm going to get dressed. Will you take the food out of the bedroom? I think I'll stick with toast and water this morning."

"Okay," he says, rushing back into the room.

I force myself to stand and pull on a robe. When I walk out of the bathroom, he's opening the windows to let out the smell of the breakfast he cooked. On the bed is a tray, only holding a bottle of water and a small plate with two slices of toast. I crawl back up onto the bed and take a long drink. I know my body needs water after losing everything inside my stomach.

Callan crawls up onto the bed, lying next to me. "How long has this been going on?" he asks, worried and confused.

I laugh. "For the past week. Usually, it's just nausea, but today it was just overwhelming. Hopefully, I can keep this toast and water down."

"If you can't, we need to contact your doctor. I know morning sickness is normal in a pregnancy, but you have to be able to keep down water."

I nod. "It usually only lasts the first hour I'm awake. I'm sure I'll be fine, and we can start our day soon."

"I'm not worried about starting our day, Val. I just want you feeling better." He reaches out and rubs my arm.

"Go take your shower and I'll eat this toast. I'm sure I'll feel better soon, and we can get going."

"You sure?" he asks, nervousness written across his handsome face.

I smile and nod. "I'm sure."

He leans forward and presses a kiss to my forehead before standing and walking into the bathroom.

I choke back my toast and finish my water. When I hear the water shut off in the bathroom, I stand up slowly, not wanting to make myself sick again by getting up too quickly. I lean against the bed until I'm sure I'll be okay, then head for the closet to pull on some clothes.

I slide into a pair of black yoga pants, noticing in the mirror how I fill them out more than before. My hips seem to be widening, my ass seems to be growing, and my stomach, while still pretty flat, is pooched out more than it ever has.

Callan steps into the closet and sees me inspecting my body. "You're beautiful," he says, coming to a stop behind me. He leans his head down and presses a kiss to the top of my shoulder.

I smile. "It's weird how it's only been a month since we found out, and already I'm seeing little changes."

He wraps his arms around me, hands resting on my stomach. "You're breathtaking. Even more so now."

I spin in his arms and wrap my hands around the back on his neck. "I hope you keep that same thought process when I'm nine months pregnant and peeing when I laugh."

He lets out a deep laugh. "Nothing is going to change my mind, Val." He presses a kiss to my lips as his feet begin walking me backward. When my back hits the wall, I break the kiss and look into his blue eyes.

"I thought you didn't want to spend all day in bed?"

He laughs. "I don't, but my mind always changes when I'm touching you." He pulls away and drops his towel as he pulls on some clothes. "Let's get all your stuff packed and then go have a lunch date. Maybe by then, you'll be hungry."

We finish getting dressed, and he drives us over to my Mom's house. The moment we walk in, she's up off the couch, giving us both a big hug.

"I can't express how happy I am for the two of you." She smiles on us fondly. "I always knew if you two could put aside your differences, you'd create something special."

Callan laughs. "Yeah, it just took me a little longer than usual to worm my way into her heart."

I playfully smack him with the back of my hand. "And to think, all it took was you being nice to me instead of torturing me," I joke.

Mom shakes her head. "You two still bicker like an old married couple. Come on, let's sit down and have some tea." She doesn't give us an option. She just leads us both to the kitchen where she fills the teapot.

Callan and I sit at the breakfast table and watch her move about the kitchen.

"So, tell me. What's the next step for you two?"

"Well, Mom, we're actually here today to pack up the rest of my belongings so I can move in with Callan full time."

She smiles as she looks over her shoulder at me. "That's wonderful. But you know, you could've just called me, and I would've hired movers for that. No need for you two to waste a whole day."

"Callan wanted to do it himself," I tell her.

"When is the wedding? Before or after the baby?" she asks, sitting down two cups of tea for Callan and me.

We look at one another. "Ugh, we haven't really talked about the wedding just yet, Momma."

She takes her seat across from us. "Take it from me: plan it for after the baby, dear. If you try getting married while you're pregnant, you'll be changing dresses three different times with that growing belly of yours." She picks up her cup and takes a sip.

"Well, actually..." I say, eyes flashing back and forth between her and Callan. "We haven't even talked about having a wedding. We could just elope." I shrug one shoulder as I look over at him.

His brows raise like he hasn't even thought of that.

"Oh, how romantic. That's how your father and I got married, you know?"

I shake my head. "I didn't know that. You and Daddy eloped?" It feels like my jaw drops.

She nods. "Your grandmother had a fit when he told her he was going to ask me to marry him. I was poor, you know. She didn't think I'd fit well in the family. So, he asked me, and we ran off that weekend to get married. When we came back, your grandparents were mad as all get out. But, there was nothing they could do. We were already legally married, and we didn't sign a prenup. If they forced us apart, they knew I could take more than my fair share." She smiles like she still enjoys thinking about pulling one over on them.

I laugh, and so does Callan. He reaches over and picks up my hand.

"Eloping sounds fun," he says, smile still in place.

I nod. "It does, actually. Just us, no big fancy wedding, no stupid dress, or spending a ton of money on flowers that will just die anyway."

"So?"

I nod. "Let's do it!"

Mom smiles and claps her hands together. "How wonderful. I'm sure you two will have so much fun. Just don't tell anyone until after you get back."

"What? Why?"

"I've already overheard Maddie and that friend of hers planning your wedding."

I laugh. "I'm surprised that you're supporting this, to be honest. I thought you'd want to be a part of your only daughter's wedding day."

She waves her hand through the air. "I'm glad someone is following in your father's and my footsteps. Bennet did the big wedding thing. It's overrated, and I'd rather see the two of you put all that money toward something good instead of a party. I've always found it to be quite frivolous."

Mom finishes her tea and excuses herself to take her midmorning nap. "Please, wake me before you go," she says, leaving the kitchen.

Callan and I stand, and I lead him downstairs to where my room is. Luckily, none of the furniture is mine. I have nothing more than some clothes, bathroom necessities, and a few mementos from my life that I've managed to hang on to.

As I'm walking into my room, Callan reaches out and catches my hand in his. He pulls me against his chest so that we're eye to eye.

"Remember that night that I snuck down here?"

I nod and smile. "Of course I do." I wrap my arms around his neck.

"Did you ever think then that this is where we'd be, getting married with a baby on the way?"

I laugh. "Hell no. Sometimes, when I wake up, I'm scared to open my eyes in fear that this has all been a dream. I'm scared that if I open my eyes, I'll find myself alone in my bed."

He shakes his head as he slowly leans in for a kiss. "This is a dream, but it's one we'll never have to wake up from," he whispers just as his lips press against mine.

His soft lips move with my own for several long moments before his tongue demands entrance. My eyes flutter closed, enjoying the way he stirs the emotions inside of my body. It feels like everything goes numb and begins to tingle to the point of tickling. Every nerve ending lights and burns bright. Holding on tight around his neck, I jump up against him, and he catches me with two hands on my ass. Without having to ask or be told, he lowers us to the bed.

I smile to myself as he kisses his way down my body. Might as well put this room to good use one last time.

His hips are grinding against mine already, and neither of us has lost our clothes yet. His strong hands massage my body as his lips kiss lower, pushing and pulling clothing out of the way. When he rips off my jeans, he slides two fingers inside of me, and his tongue flicks against my aching clit. My eyes flutter closed at the same time my lips part with a heavy gasp. My hips begin lifting on their own, moving back and forth with his tongue. I never want to separate. I need him right where he is for the rest of my life.

When my release begins to build, he pulls away, leaving me hanging.

"Hey," I cry out as he moves back up my body.

He grins. "What's the matter, Val?" he asks, sliding deep inside of me, filling every last inch.

I can no longer complain. My head falls back against the pillows as my eyes close. His mouth finds mine just as he begins to thrust in and out of me. God, I love the way he fills me completely. It's like his body was made to fit mine. It's like we were made to be a couple. He knows every spot to touch, every place to caress. I never thought we made much sense, but now, I can't see myself with any other man. Callan Gregory is it for me.

I know we should make this quiet and quick, but I don't want to. I want to take our time, feel every touch, every emotion that we cause one another to feel. I want to feel like I'm being pushed to the edge of the earth, nearly ready to fall, only to be pulled back again. I want that process repeated and repeated until I can't stand it anymore. I want to feel like a tornado is wreaking havoc on my body. Like I never know which direction it's going to go, which path it's going to take. I love the way he keeps me on my toes, never knowing what move he's going to make or what he's going to say.

"You're so fucking perfect, Val," he whispers against my skin. "God, just sliding into you makes me want to come undone." He thrusts inside of me again, this time deeper.

I call out, causing him to repeat the move; this time, he rocks his hips when he can go no further. My body tightens and prepares for my release.

"Callan, I'm going to come," I cry out quietly so that we don't wake my mom.

He doesn't stop. "Shhhh, not so loud. Your mom will hear," he whispers, turning his head to look at the ceiling.

My nails dig into his back, and I open my mouth to let out the moan that's dying to escape, but he presses his mouth to mine, causing me to whimper into his mouth.

"Fuck," he moans quickly just as his release builds and breaks free, spilling into me.

His hips slowly still, and he rests his head against my chest. "Your heart is pounding like crazy," he says.

I giggle. "It's all your fault."

He lifts his head and looks deeply into my eyes. "I love you, Val. More than you'll ever know. More than I could ever express."

I can't hold back the smile his words cause. "Me too, Callan. I don't have the words to explain how much you mean to me."

He doesn't say anything, he just gives me a soft kiss, then lays his head back against my chest so he can hear how crazy my heart is going for him.

22

CALLAN

ONE MONTH LATER...

TODAY MARKS Val's sixteenth week of pregnancy and the morning sickness hasn't slowed down a bit. Every morning, she lays in bed or sits on her knees in front of the toilet while I get ready for work. While she showers, I make her toast and get her a bottle of water. We have to get up an hour early just so she feels decent enough to go to work. But today, the sickness doesn't seem to be going away. She insists on going in anyway.

We're in the car, stuck in morning traffic on our way to the office. Her eyes are closed as she leans her head against the window. I reach over and take her hand in mine.

"You know, there is no reason for you to be putting yourself through all of this. I know this isn't the job of your dreams. Why do you keep forcing it?"

Her eyes pop open as she rolls her head to the side to look at me. "Because I'm an adult. I need a job. Women everywhere work while pregnant."

I nod. "I know they do, but it's because they have to or because they're working their dream job and don't want to miss a minute of it. Neither of those are the case for you. I mean, you haven't slept in a single day. What if, this whole time, you could've been sleeping through your morning sickness hours. Maybe a little extra rest will do you some good. I'm sure you and the baby could both use a little extra sleep. I read somewhere that your pregnant body does more work while you sleep than a normal man's body does all day with a full day of work. Your only worry needs to be growing this baby to be strong and healthy."

She offers up a weak smile. "But what about you? That would leave you short-handed at work."

I wave her off. "I'd gladly pick up the extra work if it meant that you'd be home resting."

She nods. "Okay. I'll go in today, gather my things, and tell everyone goodbye."

I smile and kiss her hand that I'm still holding. "Good. Tonight, you can go to bed early and sleep late tomorrow. Hopefully, we just figured out the key to allow you to keep down the contents of your stomach."

Traffic begins to move, and I drive on, never letting go of her hand. When we get to the office, Val gets busy on today's work. She brings me a cup of coffee even though I insisted weeks ago she stop. I don't want her on her feet more than she has to be. She goes through my mail, returns phone calls and emails, then sets to checking messages. All the while, I sit at my desk, watching her do everything but gathering her things.

"Val, I will check the messages. You, get a box from the supply room and start packing. I'm taking you home at lunch. We can eat together, and when I come back to work, you can take a nap. How's that sound?"

She leans her head back against her chair. "Amazing. I know I slept a full night, but I'm tired already, and I've only been up for three hours."

"If you're tired, it just means you need more rest. Stop pushing yourself so hard."

When lunch rolls around, I carry her box of things to the garage and place it in the trunk before climbing behind the wheel.

"What are you thinking for lunch? You want something at home, or should I swing by someplace and grab whatever you're craving?"

She looks at me with a smile. "I already called in our lunch order at Sammo's."

I laugh and shake my head. "You're never going to get enough of that place, are you?"

"Not any time soon. Every morning, I wake up craving their buffalo wings covered in ranch dressing and their Cajun chicken pasta. I don't know what it is, but this baby likes spicy foods, even if it does give me heartburn."

I grab our food and then drive us home. I carry in her box and the bags of food she ordered. "My God. How much food did you order?" I ask, walking toward the door with my arms full.

"I ordered wings, nachos, mini burgers, cheese sticks, and then both of our meals. I couldn't decide on an appetizer, so I ordered them all."

I laugh and shake my head. "Of course you did."

We take all the food to the couch, and she has it all spread out across the coffee table when I come back with two plates, forks, and water. Instead of sitting on the couch, she sits on the floor, between the couch and coffee table. She keeps her attention on the TV show she picked and the food she's eating, but I can't keep my attention off of her. Even with buffalo sauce smeared across her face, she's absolutely breathtaking. She makes my heart skip a beat and makes me feel as if I'm floating off into space. I now know what it's like to be genuinely happy, and it's all because of her.

I eat the steak she ordered me along with the freshly steamed vegetables and watch as she eats a little of everything. When she finishes, she crawls up onto the couch and lays down.

"I ate way too much."

I snicker to myself as I clean up the food. When I come back from the kitchen, she's sound asleep. I bend down and press a kiss to the top of her head. "I love you. I'll be home from work in a few hours," I whisper.

She offers up a small smile, but she doesn't open her eyes or speak. I slip out the door, locking it behind me.

———

FOR THE NEXT TWO WEEKS, I leave her to sleep in while I go to work. Every day, she tells me about spending her days, eating, swimming, and napping. On several occasions, she has dinner on the table when I get home, and she often tells me about how good she's feeling: no more morning sickness and she has so much more energy with all the extra rest she's getting. What I don't tell her is how tired I am from not only doing my job, but hers too since I haven't replaced her at work yet. I've been looking over applications but haven't yet decided on one. Nobody will do the job like she did, and to be honest, I'm not looking forward to spending all day with another woman in my office. It makes me wonder how in the hell I ever did it before her.

I leave work at lunch and swing by the house to pick up Val. She's up, dressed, and has her hair and makeup done. She's glowing. She's smiling with excitement at the hopes of finding out the sex of our baby. Her blue eyes are shining bright, and now that her belly is rounded, she looks sexy in a whole new way.

I always wondered how men felt when their hot wives gained weight during a pregnancy. My number-one reason to avoid having children before was that I was worried that I'd no longer have any interest in the woman I was with. But with Valerie, seeing her carrying around our growing baby, it makes me want her more. I love being able to put my hand on her stomach and feel the baby kick. I love feeling it move when I put my lips against it and talk to him or her. I love sleeping with one hand on her stomach. It makes me feel like I'm protecting her and our baby all with one hand. And here libido is on high alert, always down for a long fuck or a quick romp. She keeps me worn out but in a good way. I couldn't ask for more.

"Do you hope it's a boy or a girl?" she asks, glancing at me from the passenger seat.

I shrug. "It doesn't matter to me. As long as it's healthy."

She scoffs and rolls her eyes. "I hate when people say that. When you think about our future, do you see yourself playing catch in the backyard with a boy or having tea parties and playing dress-up with a little girl?"

I laugh. "I think it's twenty-nineteen and I can do both of those things with a boy or a girl." I look over at her and smirk.

She laughs and shakes her head. "I kind of want a girl. I want to dress her up in frilly dresses, paint her nails, fix her hair. I picture going for mommy-daughter mani-pedis, going to Starbucks and getting me a coffee and her a hot chocolate. Watching as she grows from a baby, to a child, to a teenager, and then an adult. Passing on my wisdom, the kind of things only a girl needs to know. Helping her recover from her first broken heart and sharing stories about all the men I left with broken hearts." She smiles, and her eyes glaze over like she's picturing everything she's listing off.

I pick up her hand and press a kiss to the top. "I hope we have a little girl too. It sounds like you have too many plans to cancel now."

She looks at me with a smile. "Yeah, but it's the same way with a boy. I picture teaching him to be gentlemen, watching him take his date to prom and not having to worry about raising a grandchild," she laughs out. "Everything from his first smile to my last."

I park the car at the ultrasound office. "Well, let's go inside and find out."

She nearly jumps from her seat and drags me to the door.

We quickly check in and have a seat in the waiting room. The whole time, her legs are bouncing uncontrollably. She picks at her pink nail polish and nervously bites her lower lip.

I place my hand on her thigh, and her legs settle down. I then place my hands over hers to stop her fidgeting, then I lean forward and kiss the lip she's biting.

"Calm down. All questions will be answered soon," I whisper against her lips.

She nods and takes a deep breath.

"I love you, Callan."

"I love you too," I reply.

"Ms. Windsor?" a lady says from behind us.

I turn and look over my shoulder at the woman standing with a chart in her hands and an open door behind her. I spin back to Val.

"Are you ready?"

She nods.

I stand up and hold out my hand. She takes it, and I lead her to the door, where we follow behind the nurse. She takes us into a private room. The lights are dimmed low.

"Please have a seat and the technician will be with you soon." She closes the door behind her, leaving us alone.

Val sits on the edge of the bed and looks around while I stand at her side.

"We haven't talked much about this moment. Are we going to tell everyone, or are we going to have some cheesy gender reveal party?"

She rolls her eyes. "I think we should just send out a group text." She laughs.

"We need to plan your bridal shower too," I state.

Again, her eyes roll. "I hate things like that."

"What? Every woman looks forward to her bridal shower."

"I hate being the center of attention." She turns and lays back on the bed. "Plus, those things are for people that can't afford to buy everything on their own. I think we have everything we need, don't you?"

"Of course, but it's a way to celebrate this new life we're starting."

"Fine, call Maddie and have her plan my shower," she agrees reluctantly.

I laugh and kiss her forehead just as the door opens.

"Ms. Windsor?" the woman asks as she sits down behind the machine.

"Yes. I'm Valerie. How are you?"

The nurse smiles. "Great. Are you ready to find out what you're having today?"

"So ready," she says, pulling up her shirt and pushing down her pants to her hip bones.

"Now, before we get started, I just want to warn you that you may leave here without knowing. It all depends on how the baby is developing and how it's laying."

Val nods. "I understand."

"Okay, let's get started." The nurse squirts some clear jelly on her stomach and smears it around with a paddle. Finally, the wall in front of us lights up, and the baby's image is projected.

It feels like the breath has been stolen from my lungs. I can see the outline of the baby's head, it's torso, arms, legs, hands, and feet. I can hear the heartbeat; it's the most beautiful sound I've ever heard. Finally, she moves the paddle, and the baby rolls over.

"I know the sex of the baby," the technician says. "Are you ready?"

Valerie looks up at me and places her hand in mine; with a gentle squeeze, she looks back and the nurse and nods her head.

23

VALERIE

"**I**s it a girl?" I ask.

The nurse smiles and nods. "It's a girl!"

We both cheer and quickly kiss as a way to celebrate. The nurse says a few things that I completely ignore because I'm so happy and blinded by the image of my baby on the wall. The machine gets shut off and then she's handing me a couple pictures she snapped of today's session.

"You can leave when you're ready," she says, wiping my stomach clean and leaving the room.

I fix my pants and my shirt and sit up, dangling my legs over the edge of the bed. I show Callan the pictures.

"Can you believe how beautiful she is already?"

He flips through them, nodding. "I can. She takes after her mommy."

He pulls me up into his arms and kisses me, long, slow, and deep.

"Come on. Let's get out of here so we can tell the rest of the family the good news." He takes my hand and leads me from the room. The whole walk to the car, I can't look at anything other than the pictures of our daughter in my hand.

IT'S GOING on ten at night, and we're both lying in bed. The pictures of the baby are still in my hands. I can't do anything but flip through them over and over. I don't know how I can tell from this crappy black and white picture, but I can see a little bit of both Callan and me in her. She looks like she will have my eye shape, but his strong jaw and chin. She looks long too; maybe she'll be tall like her daddy. I can't do anything but smile. Is it possible to be this in love with someone that hasn't even been born yet? Already, I'm so proud of her and know that she's going to be an amazing person. All I can think about is the remarkable things she'll do and the good person she's going to become.

Callan leans over and takes the pictures from my hands. "Come on. Enough of this for tonight. Let's get some rest."

I allow him to take the pictures, and I curl into his side. "How's work been going?" I ask, laying my hand on his chest.

"My new assistant starts tomorrow. I'm not looking forward to it."

"You replaced me already?" I ask, looking up at him.

He laughs. "I didn't want to, but Bennet made me when things started piling up. He hired someone on a temporary basis in case you want your job back after the baby is born. But I've been thinking, why don't you go back to the gallery you love so much?"

I scoff. "Because that was a dead-end job that didn't pay anything."

"So? I make enough money for the both of us, and you loved it so much. I mean, you almost didn't want to give it up."

"I don't want you supporting me, Callan," I breathe out as I turn my head upward to see his blue eyes shining.

His hand covers mine, and he squeezes it gently. "Val, I want you to be happy. Sitting at a desk in an office won't do that. And eventually, you'll need to escape this house. I'm just trying to think ahead. I don't want you feeling like you need to escape. I want this house to be your refuge. I want you to want to be here, run here when things out there get too crazy. Not the other way around."

"I have been here a lot lately," I agree.

He nods. "You have been. You need to get out and enjoy your free time until the baby comes."

I smile. "I'll swing by there tomorrow."

He laughs and hugs me. "Good."

———

I WAKE in the morning and Callan has already left for work. I'm so used to sleeping in now that I don't wake when he kisses me goodbye. I yawn and stretch before climbing out of bed. I walk directly to the bathroom for a shower. When I get out, I pull on my robe and head downstairs to get a cup of coffee and find something for breakfast while I look over my schedule for today. Most days, I have nothing, but I've been trying to get myself to do things more often now that I'm starting to feel better. Some days, I schedule a mani or pedi, others I'll tell myself to shop for baby clothes or diapers. Really, just anything to get out of the house for a little while.

I pour a cup of coffee and take a sip, scrunching my nose when I taste the decaf coffee Callan switched us to. While I try talking my taste buds into accepting the gross coffee, I open the fridge and find something to eat. I warm up a waffle and top it with whipped cream and strawberries. Taking everything to the breakfast table, I have a seat and open my calendar. I skim through the month until I find today's date. It looks like I have an appointment with an interior decorator for the nursery. Excitement washes over me. The appointment is at two, so I'll have plenty of time to swing by the gallery beforehand.

I'm climbing into my car an hour later. I hit the interstate, and of course, I'm stuck in lunchtime traffic. I turn the radio up louder and sing along as I move forward inch by inch. It takes me almost thirty minutes to hit my exit, but when it's in my sight, I stomp the gas and shoot across two lanes, until I'm free of the traffic jam. I glance down at the dash, finding that it's going on one already. The interior decorator is only a few blocks away from the gallery, so I will swing by the gallery and then walk to my meeting down the road, so I don't have to worry about traffic and finding parking again.

Stepping out of the car, I pull my purse up over my shoulder as I glance around at everyone busy walking and riding bikes through the city. I breathe in deep, remembering the feeling of being young and broke but living what was then my dream life. I worked around beautiful art all day. I had the most intellectual conversations with people that had the same interests as me. It's something that I didn't even realize that I missed this much.

I push through the door, and a small bell above it rings.

"Be right there," someone calls out from the back. I know that voice. It's Krista.

She comes rushing out, and her eyes grow wide as her mouth drops open. "Val? Look at you," she says, motioning toward my expanding belly.

I laugh. "I know. How have you been? I haven't seen you in a while." I lean in and give her a hug.

"Good. Keeping busy around here. What are you doing here?" She takes my hand and pulls me over to the counter and nearly pushes me to sit down.

I wiggle myself up onto the stool and place my purse on the countertop. "I'm doing good. I no longer work at the office."

"What? Why? Are you and Callan still together?" Worry paints her face.

I laugh. "Oh, yeah. We're great. I was just having a lot of morning sickness. But that's mostly passed now, and I was thinking about coming back to work here. I mean, it's not like I need the money, just something to do."

"I'm sure Jack would love to have you back, but he's not in right now. He just ran out to deliver a piece and to pick us up some lunch."

"Mention it to him, would you?"

She nods. "Of course. Gina just quit last week, so I'm sure he's wanting to fill her spot."

"What? Why did she quit? I never thought she'd leave this place.

Did they break up?" Gina and Jack had been together for nearly ten years, and they've run this place together since they opened it.

Her eyes grow wide as she nods her head up and down. "It was a big mess. I guess Gina walked in on Jack. He was in the backroom, showing a customer a piece. Well, he was showing her more than a piece... more like the piece. And she was down on her knees admiring it, if you know what I mean." Her lips turn upward at the corners.

"What?" I feel my eyes stretch wide as my mouth drops open.

She nods. "I know. So crazy."

"I always thought they were so in love. How could he do that?"

She shrugs. "I don't know. I think they must have been having problems at home. She wanted to grow up, get married, and have children. But you know Jack. He didn't want to conform to social standards. He wanted to live off the land, make art all day, all that hippie-dippie crap. Apparently, he also wanted an open relationship, and Gina wasn't having it."

I shake my head, feeling a little let down. I'd always thought they were perfect for each other.

I look down at my watch and see that it's nearing two. I stand and pull my purse back over my shoulder. "I'm sorry to rush off, Kris, but I have an appointment down the street, and it will probably take me an hour to walk there with this waddle I have going on. Talk to Jack for me?"

She smiles and nods. "Of course. I'll call you later."

I wave as I push myself forward out the door.

I'm walking into the building at two on the dot. I'm shown to a back room where a woman is already sitting at a black glass-top table with pictures scattered around.

She looks up with a smile. "Hi, I'm Simone. You must be Valerie."

I shake her hand before sitting. "I am. It's nice to meet you."

"Are you ready to design your new baby's room?"

Excitement washes over me as she beings showing me pictures and ideas of how we can design it.

I'm walking back into the house two hours later, and Callan is already home and in his office. I stick my head in to make sure he's not with a client.

"Hey," I say, walking in deeper. "Why are you home so early?"

He looks up at me, and I can see the seriousness on his face, but it falls quickly as he stands to give me a kiss. "I just decided to work from home today. Where have you been?" he asks, sitting down and pulling me onto his lap.

"I went by the gallery and found out that they're needing to fill a position, but Jack wasn't there for me to talk to. Kris is going to talk to him and give me call later. And then I went to the meeting I had with the interior decorator for the baby's room. She had some really good ideas, and I think I'm going to hire her, if that's okay."

"Of course it's okay," he says with a smile.

I lean in and give him a quick kiss. "I'm going to go upstairs and put on something a little more comfortable. What are you feeling for dinner tonight?" I ask, standing from his lap.

He loosens his tie and shrugs. "Whatever. Do you want to go out or stay in?"

"Either," I answer, moving toward the door. "I think I'm going to go for a swim." I smile at him from over my shoulder as I leave the room.

I go directly to the pool and start stripping out of my clothes. When I'm completely bare, I walk down into the heated pool slowly. I dip under the water to get my hair wet and to keep it back out of my face. When my head breaks the surface, my eyes open and land on him. He's standing off to the side, eyes locked on me as he strips out of his clothes.

I smile. "Joining me?"

He smiles and nods.

"What about all that work you had to do?"

"Fuck it," he says, just before he runs and dives into the pool.

When he comes up, he's directly in front of me, pulling me closer. I wrap my legs around his hips and my arms around his neck, pulling him in for a long, slow kiss. He walks me backward until I feel the concrete wall of the pool against my back. His hands move up to cup my cheeks as he deepens the kiss.

I can't help the small whimper that leaves my lips when I feel him harden and press against my core. His lips break free as he begins kissing down my jaw and across my chest.

"I love you, Valerie," he whispers against my skin.

"I love you, Callan," I reply, eyes closed, enjoying the way his mouth feels against my skin. We hold one another, kissing and touching until it all becomes too much.

"I need you," I whisper, breaking our kiss.

His jaw tenses and his Adam's apple bobs as he closes the distance between us against with another kiss. He picks me up against him and walks us out of the pool, but we don't go far. Instead of him carrying me up to the bed, he lays me back on a deck chair. He covers my body with his, and he fits against me perfectly. I open my legs wider, needing to feel him, and he rolls his hips, sliding into place.

It only takes seconds of him moving inside of me before I'm shattering into a million pieces. Moments later, he follows along behind me until we're melting into a puddle and mixing together.

24

CALLAN

THREE MONTHS LATER...

"Are you sure you're feeling up to going to the gallery today?" I ask Val as I dress for work.

"I'll be fine. It's nothing serious. Just my back and hips—all normal pains when you're thirty weeks pregnant." She pulls on a long, loose skirt and then pulls on her white lacy top that she hates so much.

I watch her as she stands back and looks herself over in the mirror.

"Ugh, I look like a fat cow!" She scrunches up her face when she sees her reflection.

I chuckle but move up behind her, kissing her neck as I rub her belly. "You look beautiful."

"No, I look like I just won a hotdog eating contest. I mean, look at this." She spins around to face me. Her stomach is touching mine, but she's still a good distance away from me. "To kiss you, I actually have to lean over."

I laugh. "Ten more weeks, Val. You can make it." I lean forward and kiss her long and hard. My hands find her ass, and I squeeze, causing a part of myself to come alive.

"How can you even get hard right now?" she whines against my lips.

I chuckle. "You're breathtakingly beautiful. When I see your stomach, I don't see its size. I see us, our love, our passion, our determination to be together. I love every inch of you. If I could, I'd spend all day worshiping this body." I place my hand on her stomach and rub it gently, feeling the baby kick against my palm.

She offers up a sad smile. "Please, never stop talking to me like this. I don't know how you do it, but you turn even the worst things into something beautiful."

"You're beautiful, and your stomach is beautiful, and this baby, she's going to be beautiful too." I offer her one last kiss. "Now, let's finish getting dressed so we can get to work."

"Don't forget, we're meeting Simone for dinner tonight to finalize the plans for the baby's room."

"I won't forget," I tell her, pulling on my jacket.

"Do you want me to meet you there, or should we ride over together?"

I shrug. "Whatever you want to do. I should be off work in time."

"Okay, I'll call you later and let you know how my day is looking."

I lean over and give her a kiss. "I love you."

"I love you too," she says, kissing me back.

I grab my briefcase and head out. When I get to the office, Joy is at her desk.

"Good morning, Mr. Gregory," she says, standing and rushing to get me my morning coffee.

I shrug out of my jacket and take my seat just as she's coming back into the room with my cup. "Here's your coffee, and I've already checked the messages. Anything important I wrote down and set right here," she says, reaching across my desk to touch the paper. The only problem is, her low cut top falls slightly, giving me a straight shot down her shirt.

I lean back. "Thank you, Joy."

She smiles and nods, proud of herself. "Is there anything else I can do for you, sir?" She places her hands behind her back, causing her chest to stick out a little more.

I clear my throat. "No, I'm fine. Thanks."

She smiles and nods her head, but then retreats to her desk.

When lunch rolls around, I give her my order, and she rushes out the door to get it. Bennet walks in and sits down across from me. "How's my sister and niece?"

I smile and nod. "Baby is good, growing like she should be. But your sister is getting extremely annoyed by nothing fitting and all the aches and pains."

Bennet laughs. "Valerie has never weighed more than a hundred and ten pounds soaking wet, so I'm sure this is a big change for her. She's almost done though."

"That's what I keep telling her. I'd do it for her if I could."

The door opens, and Joy walks back in. She places a bag on my desk, then starts digging through it. "Good afternoon, Mr. Windsor," she says, pulling my food out.

Bennet and I both watch her as she unwraps my sandwich and lays it flat on my desk. Next, she pulls out my fries and spills them onto the paper next to my sandwich. Finally, she opens each ketchup packet and squeezes it out next to the fries.

"Um, thanks?" I say when she finishes and stands back, waiting for approval.

She nods and leaves the office to enjoy her lunch.

"She always do that?" Bennet asks, motioning toward my lunch.

I feel my eyes stretch wide as I shake my head. "I really miss having Val here. Hell, she'd just throw me my lunch from across the room." I laugh.

"Other than this weird lunch thing, is she good at her job?" he asks, stealing a fry.

I take a bite of my burger. "She's good, but almost too good. It's annoying how on top of everything she is. And...I think she likes me," I confess.

"What do you mean?" he asks, leaning forward.

164

"I mean, she's always doing that crazy laugh, the fake one women do when they want to make a guy think he's funny. She leans over so I can see down her top. She wears extremely short skirts and then bends over to file papers in the cabinet. Once, I even saw her look over her shoulder at me to make sure I was watching. Then once, she sat where you are, and we were talking. But her knees kept getting further and further apart until I could see clear up her skirt."

His eyes nearly bug out of his head. "What? Fire her! Especially if this is getting to you. I don't want you seduced into hurting my sister."

I scoff. "I see nobody but your sister, Ben. I'm not touching that woman." I motion toward the door. "I thought maybe I could stick it out, but…" I shake my head.

"Fire her. Today. The last thing we need is for Val to come in here and see this woman flirting with you. My sister is a little unhinged normally, but with all the amped-up hormones she has right now…" He doesn't finish his sentence; he just shakes his head like he's imagining it.

I nod once. "Okay. I just didn't want you to think I was firing her for no reason. I don't have the best track record with assistants." I laugh.

———

Five o'clock rolls around, and I shut down my computer and start gathering my things. I pull on my jacket and pick up my briefcase as I head toward the door. I pause in the center of the room.

"Joy, I'm afraid I'm going to have to let you go," I say, causing her to freeze.

"I don't think this is working out. I'd like you to gather your things. Don't come back tomorrow. We'll mail your last paycheck."

I turn to leave, but the sound of her crying makes me stop and turn back around.

"I don't understand. I've been trying so hard. Why does this always happen?" she asks, walking closer to me.

I hold up my hands, palms facing her. "I…umm." I shake the panic from my head. "You're not...you don't..." I'm not sure how to put it. "I don't want to deal with you flirting with me every day. There, I said it."

She freezes. "Flirting with you?"

I nod. "Yeah, you know. The short skirts, the low-cut tops, bending over so I can see directly down your shirt or up your skirt. I mean, this is a workplace, not a club. You need to cover up, not show off your goods. I'm an engaged man."

"Engaged isn't married," she says, tears now gone as she comes to a stop in front of me.

"It is to me. I love my fiancée. We're about to have a baby together. I'm happy, and I don't need this," I motion between us, "to be misconstrued. Understand?"

She wets her lips. "Why are the good ones always taken?" She looks up, and her green eyes lock on mine.

I open my mouth to excuse myself, but the next thing I know, she's closed the distance between us. Her mouth is pressed to mine, and her hands are on either side of my face. I'm frozen in shock and fear. My eyes are wide open, staring at her eyelids as she kisses me. My hands are up in the air at my sides, palms facing her.

"Sorry I'm late," Val says, pushing through the doors.

Suddenly, I'm no longer frozen. I step back and turn toward her. The hurt on her face is evident. Her wide, glassy eyes move from me, to Joy, and back. Her lips are parted, but no words are coming out. Her right hand lays protectively on her stomach.

She shakes her head and turns, running form the office.

"Valerie!" I yell after her, but she doesn't stop.

I turn back to Joy. "Get your shit and get out. I never want to see you again," I tell her, marching toward the door.

I see the elevator doors close, but I don't have time to stop them. I rush to the elevator and start punching the buttons, needing it to stop, to open up. But it doesn't...not until she's on the ground floor and it has time to come back up.

I jump inside the elevator and hit the button for the ground level.

When the doors open, I run from the elevator and into the lobby, out the main doors, and into the parking lot. But she's gone.

Cursing under my breath, I rush to my car and get behind the wheel, driving straight home, but she isn't here. Surely she didn't go to the dinner without me. Instead of going by the restaurant, I go straight to her mom's, but her car isn't in the drive. Next, I go to Bennet's. Turning onto his street, I see her car parked in the drive. I quickly pull in behind it. I shut off the car and open the door in the same instant. I slam the door to the car closed as I push myself forward, toward the house.

I step onto the porch and pound on their door. Bennet opens it, and he shakes his head. "Come on; she's out back with Maddie."

I walk in and turn to face him. "Did you tell her? Did you tell her we just talked about this, that I don't want anyone but her?" I ask.

He nods. "I did. But she's angry and doesn't want to listen." He places his hand on my bicep and leads me down the hall to his office. "Let's just give her a moment to calm down."

"She's not going to calm down, Bennet. I have to see her now and explain."

"She's on the back porch, but I'm telling you, Cal, you need to let her calm down."

I shake my head. "No, fuck that," I mumble, throwing the door open and marching through the house. When I step onto the back porch, Maddie gives me a weak smile as she stands and walks into the house, leaving us alone. Val tears her angry eyes from mine and focuses them on the back yard.

I slowly walk over and sit in the chair Maddie just left. "Val," I start.

"No, don't Val me. I should have known. I mean, you are playboy Callan Gregory after all. You do nothing but blow through women. God, I was so stupid to think that you could change."

"Valerie," I say again, refusing to get angry. "I don't want her, or any other woman for that matter. I love you," I say, reaching out and taking her hand in mine, but she yanks it away.

"How could you do this? Have you been with her this whole time?"

"I haven't been with her at all! I love you. I want you and our baby. I fired her, and she kissed me. I panicked. I didn't know what to do. I was frozen in surprise. Before I could push her away, you were walking in."

She doesn't say anything; she just shakes her head. I'm scared to reach out and touch her again in fear that she'll push me away.

"Val, please look at me. Please, listen to me. Have I ever done anything to hurt you?"

She bites her lower lip and shakes her head.

"Then why would I start now? Now that we're finally getting everything we've ever wanted. We have the support of your family; we have a baby on the way; we're about to get married. Do you really think I'd throw all that away to fuck my middle-aged assistant? I mean, fuck. She's older than I am," I joke, and that makes her giggle.

I drop to my knees and place my hands on her hips, pulling her closer to the edge of her seat. Her hands rest on my shoulders.

"I love you, Valerie. I love you more than I've ever loved anyone. I can't live without you and our child. Please, don't throw everything away over this. I don't want her. I didn't want to kiss her. All I wanted was to fire her because she wasn't you. I don't need anything but you." I rest my forehead against hers, and when I feel her start to waiver, I press my mouth to hers, kissing her softly.

Every second that passes, the fight in her gets weaker and weaker until she's kissing me back with everything she has. Her hands push my jacket over my shoulders as she pulls me up onto her lounge chair. I settle between her legs and grind my hips against her. Her breathing is heavy and loud. It makes me want to slide into her, but her brother's back porch isn't the right place.

I break our kiss. "Please, come home with me," I beg.

She nods. "Okay."

I stand and pull her up with me. I lead her back through the house, toward the front door. Bennet and Maddie come to a stop in the foyer.

"Everything better?" Maddie asks, leaning against Bennet's side.

I smile, and she nods.

"You fired her, right?" Bennet asks.

I laugh. "Oh yeah." I tug Val toward the door. "We'll see you guys later."

We get inside my car, leaving hers here for the night, but before I can twist the key to start the car, Val is crawling onto my lap, forcing me to slide the seat back to make room for her growing belly.

"What are you doing?" I ask around a laugh.

"I can't wait until we're home. I need you inside me now." Her hands are working quickly to free me from my jeans.

"Val, we're in your brother's very lit-up driveway," I point out, but a second later, she's lowering herself onto my dick.

We both let out a relieved moan, and I can no longer hold back. I lean my seat back and place my hands on her hips as I buck up into her. She places her hands flat on my chest as she rides me back and forth, up and down.

My phone chimes from the center console and I glance at it in the darkness. It's a text from Bennet.

Are you two fucking in my driveway?!

I want to laugh, but she rolls her hips and tightens her muscles at the same time. My release builds, and her moans grow louder and louder. The next thing I know, we're both falling together.

When she takes her seat and I put myself back into my pants, I pick up my phone and send a text back.

Sorry about that.

I drop the phone back into the cup holder and start the car, taking us home.

25

VALERIE

TWO MONTHS LATER...

"CALLAN, WAKE UP!" I shake him awake when another pain rips through me.

"What? I don't want to go to the gas station again. Did you eat all those Slim Jim's already?" he mumbles, not bothering to open his eyes.

"No, Callan. I think I'm in labor," I cry out, holding my stomach

He pops up. "What? You're in labor?" He rolls out of bed and rushes to turn on the light.

I'm completely naked, wrapped in a sheet. "I think so. I've been getting these cramps every ten minutes, and they're getting more painful each time."

"Are you sure or is it like last time when you got a stomachache from topping your hot fudge sundae with spicy beef jerky?"

I roll my eyes. "I didn't eat that this time."

"You ate those Slim Jim's," he points out.

I shake my head. "I didn't eat them either. See?" I reach over and grab the six Slim Jim's off the bedside table. Only one is open, and I only took a bite out of it.

"You woke me up and made me go out and buy Slim Jim's, and you didn't even eat them?"

"Focus! I'm in labor!" I motion toward my stomach.

"Okay, well, the doctor said not to go to the hospital until your contractions are five minutes apart. So, do you want to try a warm bath first?"

I nod as I push the blankets away. He rushes around the bed to help me stand. He walks me to the bathroom and sits me down on the edge while he fills the tub. Another contraction hits me, and I double over, crying out in pain.

He rubs my back, but it's clear that he's freaked out. A sound fills my ears that sounds like a water balloon hit the floor.

"What's that?" he asks with a confused look on his face.

"I think my water broke. We have to go now. No bath." I stand, and he turns off the water. "Help me get dressed."

He helps me into a pair of sweat pants and a t-shirt. I slide my feet into a pair of flip flops and he quickly pulls on clothes and grabs my bag. We're halfway down the stairs when another contraction hits me and causes me to sit down.

I hang onto the railing of the stairs and he rubs my back, waiting it out with me. When the pain ends, he helps me stand and get to the car.

I sit in the front seat and he jumps behind the wheel. He drives like a crazy person to the hospital, calling everyone on the way.

"We're on our way to the hospital," he tells Bennet over the phone.

"Okay, we're on our way," Bennet mumbles, clearly still mostly asleep.

"Slow down!" I yell when he has to slam on the brakes to avoid hitting the car in front of us.

"These slow-ass people need to move!" he yells back, laying on the horn.

"We have time. It's our first baby. First-time labor typically takes longer. Calm down. It'll be fine," I tell him.

He laughs. "I think we have the roles reversed here."

"Oh, really? You want to have this baby?" I ask, pointing at my stomach.

He doesn't reply. Instead, he checks his mirrors and steers us off the interstate.

We make it to the hospital twenty minutes after we left the house and we're immediately given a room and a gown to change into. Callan helps me get changed and laid down in bed. Moments later, a nurse is at my side, hooking me up to machines and pulling on gloves to see how dilated I am.

"How far apart are your contractions?"

I look at Callan because I'm in too much pain to talk.

"Ugh, I guess about five to seven minutes apart. Her water broke. I do know that," he says matter of factly.

"Okay, wow. Let's see how dilated you are." She slides her hand under the blanket. "It looks like you're fully dilated. We're going to move you into a birthing room." She pulls off her glove and leaves us alone.

Callan bends forward, running his hands through his hair and breathing hard. "This is it. This is when I become a daddy. Oh my God. I'm going to have a child!" He jumps up from his chair and starts to pace back and forth.

I'd laugh if I weren't in so much pain.

He's walking back and forth, mumbling something that sounds like a pep talk—all the while, he's breathing so hard it sounds as if he's panting. He stops walking, and his facial expressions change from one of panic to one of confusion. Suddenly, he goes down.

"Oh my God! Callan!" I yell, trying to sit up.

A nurse comes running back into the room, and she drops to her knees at his side. She checks his pulse, then shines a light into his eyes. Finally, he comes to.

"Are you okay?" she asks, looking down at him.

He nods. "What happened?"

"You passed out. Stay where you are until you no longer feel dizzy," she says when he starts trying to sit up.

"I'm fine," he tells her, pushing himself to his feet. He reaches out and holds my hand.

"Are you okay?" I ask.

He nods. "I'm sorry. I'm fine," he assures me, but he looks like he has a headache or something maybe. His forehead is wrinkled, and his eyes are bloodshot.

Callan sits on the edge of the bed until a group of nurses come to wheel me into delivery.

It doesn't seem to take long before I'm in a crowded room with my legs pulled up. I'm being told to push over and over. I'm drenched in sweat. I'm tired and in pain. Every part of my body feels weak and drained.

"Okay, let's rest for a minute," the doctor says, and I relax into the bed to catch my breath.

"Put the oxygen mask on her," he orders. "You have to remember to breathe," he says, leaning over me while two nurses pull a mask onto my face.

"Doctor, her blood pressure is going up, and her oxygen is low. If she doesn't deliver this baby soon..."

"How's the baby looking?" he asks, wiping the sweat off her brow with his arm.

"The baby's heart rate is starting to fall."

Their words only make my heart race harder.

He looks at his watch. "We've been at this for hours. Let's move her into a surgery suite and perform a C-section."

"What?" I yell, grabbing ahold of Callan.

Callan leaps up. "What? Why? What's going on?"

"The long labor is wearing out both Valerie and the baby. It's too strenuous. The best option is to get the baby out now before she goes into cardiac arrest. Everything will be fine. A nurse will bring you into the room after you scrub down and change."

Without another word, I'm being wheeled away from Callan.

Something gets shoved into my IV, and before I know it, I'm relaxed and calm. I'm in no pain as I stare up at the ceiling. Callan comes into view, and he holds my hand. Even though his face is covered with a mask, I can tell he's smiling from the lines around his eyes. "Hey, how are you feeling?"

I smile. "I'm fine. How's it going down there?" I ask, eyes flashing down to the sheet I can't see past.

He leans back, gets a clear shot, and comes back. "Ugh, good?"

I want to laugh, but then I hear the baby cry.

"Congratulations, you have a baby girl," the nurse says, peeking around the sheet.

"She's here?" I ask Callan.

His smile is back in place, and he can't take his eyes off her. "She's beautiful, Val. She looks just like you," he whispers, tears filling his eyes.

Moments later, they're lying the baby on my chest. I can't tear my eyes away from her dark head of hair, her sparkling blue eyes, her chubby cheeks, and pink skin. She has the sweetest cry and the softest skin.

"Do you have a name yet?" a nurse asks.

I look at Callan, and he looks at me. "Hannah Rose Gregory," we both whisper with smiles.

———

ON ONE HAND, it seems to take forever to get cleaned up and get to our room, but on the other, it goes by in a flash. I'm lying in bed, holding baby Hannah on my chest when Maddie, Bennet, and my mom walk in.

Mom immediately comes over to steal her. She holds her close to her chest and sits down, counting her fingers and toes.

"She's so beautiful," Mom says.

"She really is perfect," Maddie replies.

I'm so tired, it's hard to hold my eyes open, but I offer a little smile. "When are you two having kids?" I ask, looking between Maddie and Bennet.

Maddie scrunches her nose. "Actually, we were just talking about taking another cruise for a couple of months."

I laugh. "How does that have anything to do with having kids?"

She shrugs her shoulder. "Every time someone has a baby, we like to celebrate not having one," she jokes.

I shake my head and look up at Callan. He leans down and presses a kiss to my forehead. "Get some rest, baby. You need it."

Before he even gets his sentence out, my eyes are fluttering closed.

————

BECAUSE OF THE C-SECTION, I'm stuck in the hospital for the next few days. But finally, we're able to go home. Callan opens the door and helps me out before crawling into the backseat to get Hannah. He fights with the car seat for a good five minutes, but finally, she's free.

"Got her?" I ask, walking toward the door.

"Yeah, this little latch thing got stuck," he replies, following me into the house.

I sit on the couch, and he places the car seat on the coffee table in front of me. She's sound asleep when he sits down. I lean my head against his shoulder, and he rests his head against mine. Neither of us can do anything but look at her, watch her sleep.

He chuckles. "She sleeps the same way you do."

"How's that?" I ask.

"You pooch your lips out like that too."

I smack his chest. "What are we going to do with this little baby?" I ask. I still find myself scared when she cries.

He shrugs. "I have no idea. I have a feeling we'll learn as she does. I mean, do any parents know what they're doing? It's all guesswork, trial and error."

I smile. "I guess you're right."

I lean forward, wanting to take her out of the car seat to hold her, but he pulls my hands back. "You get some sleep for a little while. I'll watch Hannah."

"I'm not tired," I argue.

"Then go take a shower and put on some clean clothes. Get something to eat. Let me bond with my little girl."

I smile but stand and leave them alone. I walk into the kitchen and make a pot of regular coffee. Just the thought of caffeine gets me excited. The coffee pot quickly brews it, and I pour a cup, topping it off with cream and sugar. I exit the kitchen with my cup in hand, intending on going up to the bedroom to shower and change, but pause when I hear him talking to Hannah.

"You're not going to be too tough on your dear old dad, are ya?" he asks her softly.

"You know, one of these days, Mommy's last name is going to be the same as ours. What do you think about that?"

I smile as I lean against the wall and listen in.

"As soon as we can get grandma to babysit, I'm going to steal Mommy away for a couple hours and marry her. Is that okay with you? I promise I'll bring her back. I love you and Mommy so much, Hannah."

I make my way up the stairs with my smile still in place.

EPILOGUE

CALLAN-TWO MONTHS LATER

"I don't know if I can leave her, Callan," Val whines as she places Hannah in her car seat.

"She'll be fine. It's only for a couple of hours so we can get dinner." I pick up the diaper bag and the car seat holding the baby.

Valerie pulls on her jacket and follows me to the door.

I place the car seat into the car and toss the diaper bag into the floorboard before climbing behind the wheel.

The drive to her mom's house doesn't take long but getting Val out of there without Hannah is another story. A good hour later, I pull her from the house and get her in the car. I climb behind the wheel and twist the key.

"You think she'll be okay?" she asks.

"She'll be fine, Valerie. Just relax. Breathe. Look around. It's just you and me again. Remember this?" I joke, driving to the airport.

She doesn't catch on until I'm parking the car. She looks around in a panic. "I thought we were going to dinner. What are we doing here?"

"I didn't say where we were going for dinner," I reply, stepping out of the car.

She jumps out and chases after me. "Callan, I have to be home tonight!"

"We will be. Will you just chill? Come on." I take her hand and pull her to the small private plane I rented for the day.

I greet the pilot and pay him for his services before we're shown inside the plane.

"Take off is in five. Better buckle up," he says, making his way to the cockpit.

I take the seat next to Val, and we both pull on our seatbelts. "Did you tell Mom about this?" she asks.

"Of course. And Bennet and Maddie are going to your mom's to help with Hannah. Everything is fine," I assure her.

We're given two glasses of champagne before the plane takes off.

"Are you going to tell me where we're going?" she asks, tossing the champagne back.

I laugh. "We're going to Vegas. Today is the day, Val. I can't wait another moment to make you my wife."

She smiles. "We're getting married?" she asks, tears filling her eyes.

I nod once. "That's right. Today is the day you become Valerie Gregory. Has quite the rings to it, doesn't it?"

She laughs. "Sounds a little silly. I might have to hyphenate."

I lean forward and give her a kiss.

"Why'd you wait so long?"

"I wanted to make sure you were cleared by the doctor, and that you had plenty of time with Hannah before asking you to leave her. I know leaving her alone for an hour is stressful on you. I figured leaving her to go to another state would be worse."

She reaches over and places her hand in mine. "I love you, Callan."

I lift her hand and press a kiss to it. "I love you more than you'll ever know, Valerie."

———

A FEW HOURS LATER, we're walking into the casino that also holds the chapel. I filed for our marriage license a week ago, so everything is ready to go. She's given a cheap bouquet of flowers, and I opt out of renting a tux. I'm wearing a pair of jeans and a t-shirt while Val is dressed in jeans and a flannel. I want to laugh at our appearance, but I know when I look back on this day, I'll think it's perfect. We aren't exactly a traditional couple, so why would we settle for a traditional wedding?

When the music starts and the doors open, I can't do anything but watch her walk toward me. She's beautiful, with her long, dark curls flowing down around her. She's wearing a wide smile, and her eyes are shining bright. The moment she stops next to me, I can't control myself. I have to lean in and kiss her. She laughs against my lips, but that doesn't stop her from kissing me back.

We go through the whole process of repeating our vows, and finally, I get to the slide the gold band onto her finger next to her engagement ring.

"You may now kiss your bride," the minister says, and he doesn't have to tell me twice. I pull her against me and kiss her hard and passionately.

The music starts up again, and we walk down the aisle. She turns over the bouquet, and we're handed our marriage certificate. I lead her from the chapel into the elevator.

"Where are we going? When is our flight home?"

"Not for a couple more hours. I got us a room," I say, turning to face her as I walk her backward. When her back hits the wall and she can no longer escape me, I pull her against me and kiss her like I haven't kissed her in years. Her arms wrap around my neck, pulling me closer as her thighs wrap around my waist. Keeping one hand on her ass to support her weight, I turn and walk us off the elevator when the doors open. We don't separate as I walk us down the hall and to our room.

I slide the key into the door, and it beeps, allowing me to twist the handle and walk in. I toss the plastic key card onto a nearby table, and she does the same with our certificate, then we fall into bed, wrapped in each other.

We haven't had sex since before Hannah was born. We had to wait for her to heal, and then we were both just so tired from taking care of a newborn baby, but tonight is the night. We lose our clothes at lightning speed, and before I can even think about what I'm doing, I'm sliding deep inside of her. I see fireworks behind my eyelids. Her heat and pressure are enough to have me ripping at the seams. There's no way I can leave her any time soon.

She rolls us over and gets herself on top. My hands fall on her hips, begging her to ride me faster, harder, and when I feel her muscles begin to tighten around me, I thrust up into her harder while she rocks against me. Watching her come is life-changing. She's beautiful. Her plump lips part with her heavy breathing and her loud moans. Her big chest pushes outward, making me want to suck a nipple into my mouth, and her nails dig into my chest, treading a line between pain and pleasure.

When her whimpers have quieted, I roll us back over so I can give to her some more. No way am I ready to be done. I need to be in her, feel her, taste her. I rock my hips against her body, and she can't do anything but call out my name. When my release begins to rise, I try pushing it back, but she feels too good. I have to let it go, or I know it will control me anyway. Finally, every muscle tenses and tingles take over my body. My thrusts become rushed and hard, and I let my release go, filling her as I moan against her lips.

We both freeze to allow our bodies to come back down from the high we were riding. When I roll to her side, her body curves against mine. Her hand lands on my chest, and her cheek presses against my shoulder.

"This is perfect, Callan. Thank you," she whispers.

"Thank you," I reply.

"For what?" she asks, confused.

"For everything, Val. For giving me a chance, for running to me instead of away from me back then. For giving me a beautiful daughter. For marrying me. For making me the luckiest man alive. Thank you."

She offers up a small smile. "You're welcome." She leans in and kisses me soft and slow.

"I love you," I whisper against her lips.

"I love you," she whispers as she climbs back on top of me, rolling her hips until she's sliding down my length once again with a loud moan.

We spend the rest of our Vegas time in our room. We make love over and over, then take a shower before getting dressed and going back to the airport. I can't help but watch her on the flight home. She does nothing but sleep, but it's something I've always been fascinated by. The way she breathes, the way she whimpers, the way she looks completely relaxed and happy. I know we have it all, and I could never ask for more.

The plane lands hours later, and I carry Val from the plane to the car. To my surprise, she doesn't wake when I pull up to her mom's house either. I leave the car running and lock the doors while I run in and get Hannah. I load the car seat and get behind the wheel to drive home. The entire time, both girls are sound asleep.

Getting them into the house is a bit trickier. I take Hannah first, placing her seat on the floor by the stairs while I run out and get Valerie. I carry Valerie inside and lock the door behind us. I carry her up to bed and strip off her shoes before covering her up. Then, I go back down for Hannah. When I bend down to take her out of her seat, her eyes pop open and scan the room.

"Hi, baby girl," I coo, picking her up against my chest. I carry her into the kitchen while I make a bottle, then we head up to the bedroom for the night. I change her diaper and put her into a warm sleeper before sitting down in the rocking lounge chair to feed her. My girl has an appetite, and she sucks down the bottle like usual. I burp her and lay her down in the cradle we keep by the bed. Finally, both girls are sound asleep, and I'm free to strip down and slide into bed next to my wife.

I wake several times with Hannah, repeating the process of changing her diaper, feeding her, and burping her. The whole time, Val doesn't wake. Finally, she rolls over at seven with a startled inhale.

"Good morning," I whisper from the chair while feeding Hannah.

"What? How?" she asks, looking around the bedroom. "How'd we get here? When?"

I laugh. "We got in around midnight last night. You fell asleep on the plane. I swung by your mom's, picked up Hannah, and carried you both to bed."

"I slept all night? You were up with her all night?" She stands from the bed and walks over to look down at Hannah.

"I got a few hours of sleep here and there. You must have been worn out."

"With a new baby that only sleeps for an hour at a time, the travel, and the sex, yeah, I was tired," she laughs. "How about I start breakfast since you took the baby shift last night?"

I nod. "Sounds good. I'm going to lay her down and jump in the shower. I'll be down soon."

She smiles and nods before walking out.

I finish up with Hannah, lay her down, and turn on the baby monitor so Val will hear her if she cries. Then I step into the shower, and the hot water instantly relaxes me. I can't say that it wakes me though. If anything, it relaxes me to the point of needing to sleep. I don't know how Val does it—keeps up with this crazy sleeping routine. From the moment Hannah was born, I've never woken with her. Valerie's always insisted that she wanted to do it. After last night, I will now insist on helping her throughout the night. That's entirely too much for one person to handle on their own.

I step out and pull on a pair of sweat pants before checking on Han and heading downstairs to find Val platting up the eggs, bacon, and toast. She has coffee ready, and two glasses of orange juice already poured and waiting on the breakfast table. I help her plate the food and I carry out plates to the table while she pours two cups of coffee. Finally, we're able to sit down and enjoy a hot meal together.

"Thanks for letting me sleep last night," she says before taking a sip of coffee.

"I'll be doing that more often."

Her brows furrow together.

"I know you insist on taking care of her, but that's too much for you to do alone."

"Are you crazy? No way can you keep up a sleep pattern like that while you're working. You'll be falling asleep at your desk."

I shrug. "Oh well. I guess my new assistant will have to pick up the slack."

"Did you finally get a new one?" she asks, pushing the eggs around her plate?"

I nod. "Yeah, Maddie found her. She doesn't start until tomorrow, but she brought her to my office Friday to introduce us."

"And?" she asks.

"And, I think you'll really like her. Her name is Tracy. She's Bennet's assistant's sister. She's probably as old as our moms. She's married, has six kids, and fourteen grandchildren. She's a really sweet older lady that can keep her hands to herself," I laugh out.

Valerie joins in on my laughter. "Good. I'd hate to have to be your assistant again just because I can't trust other women around my husband."

I smile. "That's the first time you called me your husband."

"It is. Do you like the sound of it?" she asks, standing and walking around the table. She slides onto my lap, facing me.

"I do like the sound of that. But I think I like the sound of fucking my wife on the breakfast table even more."

She lets out a loud laugh that's cut off by my kiss. I stand, setting her on the edge of the table and working her oversized t-shirt up her thighs. Using one hand, I push my sweatpants down my hips and position myself at her entrance. With one roll of my hips, I'm right where I need to be, where I crave to be. Valerie wasn't something I expected, but she's something I need more than food to eat or air to breathe. Valerie is my forever, and as long as I have her and our daughter, I'll never want for anything.

It's funny how things sneak up on you. One day, you're living your ordinary life and refusing to fall in love, and then it hits you so hard, you don't know what happened. I don't know how Valerie worked herself under my skin so much, but I thank God every day that she did. I thought I had everything I needed before, but compared to now, I had nothing. It only took me twenty-five years to figure it out, but now I know what's important. It's not money, women, or a good job. It's finding that one person that knows you, understands you, and loves you for you. It's becoming friends, falling in love, and creating a family that will always have your back.

"I love you, Mrs. Windsor-Gregory," I whisper against her lips.

"I love you too, Mr. Gregory," she replies, letting her release wash over her.

READ THE REST OF THE SERIES HERE

Make Her Mine Series
My Best Friend's Brother
Billionaire With Benefits
My Boss's Sister
My Best Friend's Ex
The Friend Agreement (Coming this March)

ALSO BY ALEXIS WINTER

Hate That I Love You: Castille Hotel Series Prequel

Want this prequel for FREE? Sign up here to get it along with a second free novel delivered right to your inbox!

Castille Hotel Series

Business & Pleasure: Castille Hotel Series Book 1

Baby Mistake: Castille Hotel Series Book 2

Fake It: Castille Hotel Series Book 3

South Side Boys Series

Damaged-Book 1

Broken-Book 2

Wrecked-Book 3 (Coming December)

Redemption-Book 4 (Coming February)

Claimed by Him: A Contemporary Romance 6 Book Collection

ALL BOOKS CAN BE READ AS STAND-ALONE READS WITHIN THESE SERIES

ABOUT THE AUTHOR

Alexis Winter is a contemporary romance author who loves to share her steamy stories with the world. She specializes in billionaires, alpha males and the women they love.

If you love to curl up with a good romance book you will certainly enjoy her work. Whether it's a story about an innocent young woman learning about the world or a sassy and fierce heroin who knows what she wants you,'re sure to enjoy the happily ever afters she provides.

When Alexis isn't writing away furiously, you can find her exploring the Rocky Mountains, traveling, enjoying a glass of wine or petting a cat.

You can find her books on Amazon or at
https://www.alexiswinterauthor.com/

Follow Alexis Winter below to get awesome deals, participate in giveaways and get advanced sneak peeks of upcoming releases!